"In *Nevers*, readers will be spellbo........ ...e magic and mayhem of Odette and Anneline's life in motion. Against a rich background of post-Revolutionary France, they'll learn of perseverance, friendship and love in many forms. Cassidy is a master storyteller, and her fresh imagery and wordplay, along with a well-paced plot and a diverse cast of characters, are a real delight."

—Julie Paul, author of *Meteorites* and *The Pull of the Moon*

"*Nevers* is a marvelous and magical book with an unforgettable heroine—prepare to be transported!"

—Esta Spalding, author of the Fitzgerald-Trouts series

"Odette's drawn to the fascinating sights of Nevers, and readers will be as well…This brief sojourn in an alternative 18th-century France is an unexpectedly rich one."

—*Kirkus Reviews*

"*Nevers* is a funny story, simply told, with a delightful heroine. It has been a long time since I read such a convincing, relevant historical novel for children. Highly Recommended."

—*CM: Canadian Review of Materials*

Nevers

SARA CASSIDY

ORCA BOOK PUBLISHERS

Library and Archives Canada Cataloguing in Publication

Title: Nevers / Sara Cassidy.
Names: Cassidy, Sara, author.

Identifiers: Canadiana (print) 20190066172
Canadiana (ebook) 20190066199 | ISBN 9781459821637 (softcover)
ISBN 9781459821644 (PDF) | ISBN 9781459821651 (EPUB)

Classification: LCC PS8555.A7812 N48 2019 | DDC jC813/.54—dc23

Library of Congress Control Number: 2019934045
Simultaneously published in Canada and the United States in 2019

Summary: In this magical middle-grade novel, Odette unlocks a mysterious spell.

Orca Book Publishers is committed to reducing the consumption of nonrenewable resources in the making of our books. We make every effort to use materials that support a sustainable future.

Orca Book Publishers gratefully acknowledges the support for its publishing programs provided by the following agencies: the Government of Canada, the Canada Council for the Arts and the Province of British Columbia through the BC Arts Council and the Book Publishing Tax Credit.

Edited by Barbara Pulling
Cover design by Rachel Page
Cover artwork by Serena Malyon
Author photo by Katrina Rain

ORCA BOOK PUBLISHERS
orcabook.com

Printed and bound in Canada.

22 21 20 19 • 4 3 2 1

Pour Donald, et à la mémoire de Carol

Prologue

Here follow the adventures of resourceful, fourteen-year-old Odette and her beautiful but mortally clumsy mother, Anneline, on their arrival by cheese cart to the small city of Nevers, in a part of France where the fields are green and rolling, the houses are built stone upon stone, castles rise over the landscape and rabbits raid gardens on moonlit nights.

Radishes are especially sweet and soporific when the moon is full. Clover is too. I know these things because I know things that most mortals do not. I know the smell of clover when the moon glints like a silver coin tossed aloft by Fortune deciding whom to favor.

I tell this story because Odette is too modest to speak of herself. She is having a well-deserved rest now, and when she opens her eyes again, she will be too busy to dwell on the past. After the marvels that have exhausted her, Odette is poised to enter her own life.

Why is it that we want to know what others think and feel? To dip our buckets into their silence? Why do others' stories seem more colorful than our own? Perhaps each of us knows our own story too well. It is erased, as it were, as soon as we turn the page.

I understand what it is to yield to silence. To have words clot in your throat and to choke when you mean to speak. These days, though, words flow through me as easily as water released down riverbeds in spring. The snow has melted, and the ice has thawed. I will do my best to share all that I have seen and heard.

For a long time the people of Nevers laughed at me. They threw rocks at me, dead fish, the spokes from a broken carriage wheel once. But late at night, when they were lonely and afraid, some of them confided in me.

I will miss a few details—that is inevitable. But I'll embellish here and there to balance things out. Not to worry. The main facts of the story are sturdy. Its bones, its timbers. Time to step into its chapters. Time to set sail for a corner of France in the very last year of the eighteenth century.

One

"*W*hoa!"

W The carriage halts suddenly, startling Odette from a dream in which she was a large wheel of soft cheese about to be rolled off a cliff. She has spent several hours as a stowaway in the back of a dairy delivery carriage, with a block of Comté cheese for a pillow and a ragged length of damp cheesecloth for a blanket. Is it any wonder she is dreaming about Camembert?

Odette listens as the milkman steps down the carriage's creaky steps to the muddy road. Footsteps approach, sucking at the muck. "*Bonjour*," says the milkman. A man with a gravelly voice responds. The two discuss the unseasonal downpour that occurred just before dawn and fall into conversation about the best remedy for an aching bunion. One swears by boiled chamomile flowers mashed with leopard-slug slime. The other recommends manure from black pigs, collected in a thunderstorm.

The two strike a deal for a dozen wheels of Brie for an impending wedding feast. They then agree that it isn't too early for a glass of wine.

Odette elbows her mother, who snores wetly beside her. "We've arrived somewhere."

Anneline raises her head and scowls at the murky surroundings. She closes her eyes again. Odette raises the carriage's canvas cover a thumb and watches as the milkman hitches his horse to a post and bumbles into the tavern with his friend. Odette tugs her mother's loose braid. "Now."

"Ouch." With much grumbling, Anneline unfolds herself from the crush of cream jugs and butter logs while Odette gathers up their few belongings. Anneline points to a basket brimming with small goat cheeses. "Grab some trouser buttons. And a round of Morbier. That's the one striped with black ash."

"I won't thieve."

Odette leaps down to the mucky road and puts out her hand to help her mother.

Daylight powders the darkness. A woman in rags struggles past, pushing a wheelbarrow heaped with cauliflowers. A man lugs reed cages; inside them heavy rabbits move warily, the X's of their noses twitching for a familiar smell.

"Market day," Odette observes. "I wonder what town this is."

Anneline turns to a man draped in sausages. "Excuse me…"

Odette grabs her mother's grimy sleeve. "Mother, you can't just ask a stranger, 'Where am I?'"

"Why not?"

"It's the one thing you're supposed to know—where you are."

"I suppose. But I know a lot of things people *aren't* supposed to know, such as what a man's finger looks like lying on a paisley carpet. That toothy dog was far too protective of me. And the cruelty of nuns. And the sweet ache in a woman's lungs as she exhales her last wretched breath of air—"

"It was not your last breath of air, Mother."

"It could have been."

"Except, of course, you'd flirted with a fireman earlier that day."

"Is it my fault he fell in love? Or that he chose to dive into the cold water to save me?"

"Drowning himself."

"Yes. Poor man."

"And now you've gotten another person killed. I saw legs sticking out from the rubble. Mr. Pannet, I'm quite sure, judging by the expensive shoe leather."

Anneline giggles. "The tax collector. Finally some luck." But then, to Odette's surprise, her mother's face crimps with concern. "Was there anyone else?"

"Crushed? I don't know. I don't think so."

Anneline peels off a white glove and waves it in the air. "I surrender."

Odette grits her teeth. She has little patience this morning for Anneline's potion of charm and helplessness. "Surrender from your life, Mother?" she asks. "Not possible. Not with that dirty glove anyway."

The rising sun has cast the sky in pink, bringing light to the faces of the farmers and artisans preparing their market stalls. The shadow thrust by the massive cathedral at the edge of the marketplace begins to retreat. Odette takes in the buildings around her and glimpses in the distance a wide river busy with boats. She and her mother have arrived in a sizable town.

As they walk through the wakening marketplace, Odette remembers to keep a close eye on Anneline, who has a dismaying habit of taking fruit from the bottom of fruit sellers' carefully stacked pyramids. But Anneline isn't eyeing the fruit. Instead, she is staring up at the cathedral walls.

"Now *those* are flying buttresses!" Anneline points to the row of high stone arches that keep the cathedral walls from collapsing sideways. "I could have used a couple of them last night."

"Why *did* you push over that wall?"

"I only leaned against it. I was tired. Light-headed from the wine."

Anneline giggles, but to Odette the giggle sounds forced. Hollow. Does her mother actually feel *shame*? That would be new. And she hasn't sent apples rolling into the street, nor is she chatting with everyone they pass, flashing her white teeth. Perhaps Anneline is changing. Perhaps, Odette dares to hope, in this unfamiliar city there will be no misadventure, no chaos—

"Thief!"

A bony woman in a dirty pinafore pulls forcefully on Anneline's cloak.

"Let my piglet go!" the woman screeches.

Anneline, rattled, lifts her skirt. A glistening pink snout protrudes from underneath. "Get out of there, you silly beast!" Anneline warbles. But the piglet only disappears again beneath her petticoats.

"The rich are cockroaches," the bony woman squawks to the gathering crowd. "The Revolution did not stamp them all out."

Anneline lifts her skirt again. Odette notices that her knees are scratched from scrabbling in the castle rubble the evening before. The small pink creature snuffles at her feet.

"Oooh. Her ankles must smell like truffles," titters a large man with ink-stained fingers and an impressive nose.

Odette reaches for her mother's hand. "You need to get away from it. Jump!"

Anneline tries to hop over the piglet, but she trips and lands on the small beast, making it squeal like a set of wounded bagpipes. As the creature squirms beneath her, Anneline flails and falls backward. Her head strikes a cobblestone with a *CRACK* that echoes off the cathedral wall.

"Ohhh," the crowd murmurs.

The skinny woman in the dirty pinafore snatches up her piglet and wags a finger in Anneline's face. "Serves you right!"

But Anneline does not respond. She is unconscious.

A man who has been applying paint the color of the local red wine to a nearby window shutter hurries down his ladder and strokes Anneline's head with his paint-spattered hand. "Her ladyship, so radiant, so ravishing, so shapely," he coos.

"Hey!" Odette yells. "My mother is not shapely."

Anneline stirs. "Actually, Odette, I am. All of my husbands have said so."

"Divine angel," the painter sings. "Do you know where you are?"

Anneline raises her head and looks about, dazed. "No," she says. "I haven't ever been here before."

"I will tell you. You are in the town of Nevers."

Two

It is difficult to shake the painter. Odette finally points to the paint hardening on his paintbrush and says, "You'd better get those shutters finished."

The painter looks wounded. "It is true," he admits. "I must return to my labors." He reaches for Anneline's hand. "If you ever need something painted— a room, a wall, a bedstead—ask for Guillaume. I am at your service." He climbs back up his ladder, shouting "*Adieu!*" from the top rung as Odette and her mother head into a maze of narrow streets.

"What would *I* want with a piglet?" Anneline complains. "It was a cute little thing, though, wasn't it? Those freckles like soot spots. Oh, my head. What did that odd-looking painter call this town?"

"Nevers," Odette answers.

"It's an English word, isn't it? For nowhere? Or nothing?"

"It means 'not ever.'"

"That sounds promising. Like oblivion or something."

"Oblivion is promising?"

"From the Latin *oblivio*, meaning 'obliteration,'" says Anneline. Anneline's fourth husband had been a polyglot, a morose one, who taught the children of the wealthy and undertook to teach Odette and her mother Latin and Greek. Odette had done well, but Anneline had not—she had bristled at having to sit like a schoolgirl. "Complete forgetfulness. Wouldn't that be restful?"

"No!" Odette cries.

But maybe it would be. Odette could forget all of the calamities her mother had wrought, and her parade of awful husbands. Maybe she could forget the questions posed by her own pale, lopsided face whenever she caught sight of her reflection, questions about the "ugly husband," as her mother referred to the first husband, who had engendered her. He was a librarian who, though not dashing, was rumored to have had a half ounce of royal blood in his veins. Odette had never met him. Anneline had not learned she was pregnant until the day after he died.

"If we forgot everything, I believe I would be young again," Anneline muses. "I am beautiful now, but you should have seen me at your age, Odette. Once, in the town of Cluny, spying me from high in the tower, the abbey bell ringer was unable to ring the Angelus bell, he was so hypnotized by my elegance. It was the first time in a thousand years the bell was silent…"

An onlooker might have wondered how mother and daughter could be so at ease walking the streets of a strange town with nothing but the clothes on their backs and their worldly belongings in a single bag —which Odette carried. Inside the bag were their identity papers, a needle and thread, Anneline's face powder and Egyptian oil, Anneline's favorite book and Odette's knife.

The truth was that Odette and Anneline were practiced at being uprooted. "Time to change addresses," Anneline had announced more than a dozen times in the fourteen years since Odette was born.

When she was little Odette had cried and felt fearful when she and her mother had to move along, but for many years now she had accepted her lot. Her mother couldn't help being herself. Moving was expected. *Staying* was unexpected.

But this time is different. Odette feels it in her bones. The evening before, hiding in the bushes by the castle rubble, she had noticed stunned strands of white in Anneline's black braid and a weariness in her eyes. There was sorrow in her voice, too, possibly regret. Her mother is changing.

Odette always keeps a sharp eye on her mother. Anneline is "a danger," as one husband put it. "Accident prone," said another. She has many times been the cause of injury—or worse. Her second to last husband, a healing-salts magnate, had called her a "saboteur." At a dinner party, the president of a competing salts company had discovered Anneline's love of wine and proceeded to fill her glass over and over until she whispered her husband's recipes into the man's hairy ear. Her husband was bankrupt within a year.

Her most recent husband, Marcel, an archeologist, had thought her merely "clumsy." Well, now he had seen the full extent of her clumsiness.

Odette, Anneline and Marcel had spent nearly a year in the sleepy town of Sigy-le-Châtel, where Marcel had bought the castle ruins overlooking the town. Their restoration was to be his life project, and Anneline his helpmate.

Anneline had overseen a party the night before, which was to raise money to refurbish the ruins. She'd drawn up the menu and hired the band. (She'd arrived home from their first meeting drunk, in a hay cart pulled not by a horse but by a wild-haired musician who periodically blew into a dented French horn, sending magpies flapping out of the trees.)

The party was Anneline's vision, but Odette, of course, had kept it all afloat, delivering the invitations, ordering the food, even swinging a scythe at dawn to clear a field for dancing.

The event had been planned for a full moon, when the ruins would be "bathed in moonlight," a phrase Anneline loved to repeat. It had begun gloriously.

Silver trays polished like mirrors. Glistening oysters on thin slices of baguette. Tall glasses of fizzing champagne. Men in tuxedos, their beards trim. Women in gowns and long necklaces.

The crowning glory of the ruins was the remaining side of the castle keep. It towered over the local countryside, its ghostly remnant height enthralling. It was a marvel, nearly miraculous, that the single wall stood, unsupported stone on top of stone on top of stone. Marcel's first planned project was to bolster it. Indeed, the evening would raise the funds to do so.

The musicians were singing "*À la claire fontaine*":

> *In the clear fountain*
> *As I was strolling by*
> *I found the water so lovely*
> *That I bathed there.*
> *Long have I loved you.*
> *Never will I forget you.*

When they finished, the crowd cheered, then quieted, attentive for the next musical offering.

And it was in that moment of expectant silence that a crash like the worst thunder, like a stampede of a hundred horses, like a mountain falling, filled the air. Guests screamed. Birds screeched. Dust billowed thick as smoke.

The great castle wall of Sigy-le-Châtel had fallen. The air throbbed, swirling where it had not for centuries.

Marcel ran toward the rubble and fell to his knees, moaning. Party guests rushed to comfort him (Odette noticed that they didn't kneel in the dirt as Marcel did, but squatted so as to keep their formal trousers clean). Others clambered over the rocks, looking for casualties.

In the midst of the chaos, a length of red silk sailed over the debris. Marcel caught it and clutched it to his chest, launching into louder paroxysms of unhappiness. When Odette asked to see her mother's scarf, Marcel dabbed his eyes with it, then handed her the moist cloth.

Odette recognized immediately that what her mother's seventh husband took as a symbol of Anneline's demise was in fact a message for her, the knot in it tied *after* the wall fell and just before her mother threw it. As the partygoers scrambled over the fallen rocks, calling her mother's name into the dark openings, Odette sneaked toward the bushes at the edge of the ruins.

Odette was sure her mother would not have perished in such an outrageous accident. Outrageous accidents were how her mother *lived*. No, Odette had never doubted that Anneline would die at the end of a boring day spent playing shuffleboard and eating mashed prunes. There would be no mayhem, no murder, no mystery— just a slowing of heartbeats, a little more silence between each breath, a little less air and a little more space.

But the people in their evening gowns swinging lanterns over the rubble and crying, "Anneline! Anneline!" were fooled. For in their tidy, sleepy lives, walls did not fall. The world did not perpetually shift sideways, did not zig or zag. This was Odette's life. Turmoil was always on the horizon—when it wasn't under her feet.

Odette put the scarf to her nose and smelled the Egyptian oil that her mother rubbed into her neck each morning as she murmured, "My neck will not collapse, my neck will not collapse. My neck is not the Roman Empire." Sometimes the smell comforted Odette, but now it angered her.

A dove cooed in the bushes, sounding much like the one she and her mother and Marcel had heard that morning while eating breakfast. Only this dove was articulate.

"Coo-coo-Odette," it said.

"Coo-coo-coming," Odette grunted in reply.

Odette pointed across the heap of ancient stones and called out to the thwarted revelers. "Legs! Someone has been crushed!" It was true. As she was clambering over the rocks, she had come upon a pair of lifeless trousered legs sticking out from the wreckage.

The men and women in fancy clothes flocked across the rocks, and Odette backed into the woods until a bony hand clamped onto her shoulder. "Time to change addresses," Anneline said.

Through the dark night Odette had led her mother across fields, over streams and through forests, Anneline complaining incessantly. "My feet are so sore. I didn't eat even one oyster. Why is the moon so faint? Stop. I am out of breath."

But when they did stop, Odette felt the weight of the sky over her and the stars piercing its darkness like knifepoints, urging her to keep going and to never return.

Three

Odette and Anneline step into an alley thick with chickens squawking and scrambling over each other as a heavyset man in a cloak made of chicken feathers scatters handfuls of corn. "Feast, beautiful chickens, lucky chickens."

"Excuse us," Anneline says.

The man gazes at her wonderingly, as most men do. "M. Gustave feeds the chickens, and the chickens feed M. Gustave!" he jokes, clearly hoping Anneline will find him clever.

Odette tugs on her mother's cloak, wanting to steer her back toward the main road, but Anneline tosses her head and strides through the clot of clucking chickens.

"Mother," Odette pleads.

"Did you ladies notice the rain early this morning?" The man raises his sturdy paw of a hand. "Drops larger than my thumb! Amazing liquid!"

"Yes," Anneline agrees. "The raindrops were enormous. Large as caterpillars."

Odette bites her tongue. Her mother didn't see the rain—she snored among the cheeses as it fell.

But Odette saw it. As they had rumbled up and down the hills and valleys of Burgundy, she had pressed an eye to a hole in the carriage's canvas cover and watched happily as the glaring stars were swallowed by dark cloud. The drops that fell had indeed been unusually large.

"They leapt when they struck the ground!" M. Gustave says, his broad, red face shining with enthusiasm.

"Like sparks," Anneline says. "Fairy lightning."

M. Gustave bows. "You are most interesting, Madame."

"And you have lovely chickens."

"I do."

"I will buy one from you one day and savor its meat."

"It is good meat. Tender and moist."

"I'm sure it is," Anneline agrees flirtatiously. "My daughter and I will choose a big bird, with enough feathers for me to make a hood for your cloak, to protect you from large drops of rain."

Odette winces, knowing she will be the one to make the hood. She will be the one to buy the chicken. To wring its neck. To pluck it. To build the fire to roast it. Odette does not like to think about the promises her mother has made and broken. In her mind they lie like ribbons on a dirty road, fallen from the hair of wealthy girls bouncing along in a cabriolet.

We will get your shoes repaired in the morning.

I will trim your hair—I am very good with scissors.

I will wash the pot—don't you worry.

You'll like this one—he's very nice and smart. We'll be married forever.

At least there is another side to the ledger. Anneline has never once scolded Odette. And Odette has never disappointed her mother. She has never complained. Until now. She was happy in Sigy-le-Châtel. She'd had a livelihood there, tending a neighbor's hogs. She liked the hogs, and they liked her. Now they will think she abandoned them.

"*I* will be the one to sew the hood," she mutters, her jaw tight.

Her mother studies her, confused. "Well, yes."

"I mean..." Odette starts. "You said *you'd*..." But her body rebels at this new tack. Her skin prickles with sweat. Her mouth goes dry. She can't continue. A chicken runs past, chased by a rooster. "Never mind," she mumbles.

"My daughter and I are seeking a house to rent," Anneline tells M. Gustave. "We are new to Nots."

"Nevers," Odette says under her breath.

M. Gustave doesn't seem to care that this mother and daughter wear fancy clothes stained with mud, or that their hair is knotted, or that they smell faintly of cheese. Perhaps it is Anneline's hypnotic green eyes or her assurance that she will one day buy one of his chickens, but M. Gustave stops casting corn and sizes up the pair with interest.

"I know of an apartment," he says. "The old gatehouse. Once upon a time, anyone entering Nevers had to declare themselves to the sentry, show their papers or whatnot and explain their business.

Soldiers ran the place then, but now my hen Lisane rules the roost, ha-ha. If there is a prize for the highest-flying hen, my Lisane would win it. She flies in and out through a broken window.

"I climbed the stairs not long ago, ducked through the old door and found my Lisane strutting happily between the two small rooms. The place needs a sweep and something in the windows to keep the wind out, and maybe it's a bit noisy, with the carriages passing under all day. But there is a fireplace and even a mattress, and the roof only leaks in a few spots."

To Odette, the lodging sounds little better than a chicken coop. Still, it's worth a visit.

"The sooner we get settled, the sooner we can prepare a chicken feast," Anneline tells M. Gustave.

So M. Gustave leads Odette and her mother left and right down narrow streets and alleys until they stop at a small stone house straddling a road like a bridge. Fishmongers and carts and laughing children pass right under it.

Its window is framed with battered shutters, and the little house is slightly askew. But it isn't altogether awful, Odette thinks. It even holds some charm. It is draped with vines, which make it look cozy, and the roof slates are small and even. Odette takes a deep breath. She and Anneline may sleep well here.

M. Gustave huffs and puffs up the stone stairs. Odette imagines he must be hot in his feathered cape. "Now that I think of it, I haven't seen Lisane in quite a few days," M. Gustave says. "I hope a fox hasn't gotten in."

Odette and Anneline follow him through a small door into a small room that holds a weary mattress and a blackened fireplace. The second room is even humbler, except for a surprisingly graceful armoire on short, curved legs. Cherry wood, Odette deduces by its reddish color.

The apartment floors are littered with mouse droppings, and the thick layer of dust on the floors, windowsills and mantelpiece is etched with chicken prints. Odette decides to leave a few of the cobwebs when she cleans, in case she or Anneline cut themselves—webs are excellent for sealing wounds. This is the kind of thing a young girl with a peripatetic life learns.

Odette puts her head into the fireplace and looks up. The square of blue sky at the top of the chimney is as clear as the water at the bottom of a well.

"Well?" M. Gustave asks, still catching his breath from the short climb up the stairs. "What do you see?"

"Nothing."

"That's what you want. Rare for a chimney that has sat so long to be free of nests. A good sign. Of course, some people go ahead and light a fire even when there is a nest. The birds flap fast and high into the air with their tails smoking. It is very, very cruel."

Anneline lowers herself onto a corner of the mattress. She looks at Odette and asks meekly, "Can we stay?"

Odette nods. "We'll take it," she tells M. Gustave.

"Four francs each full moon."

"But you don't own it," Odette argues. "Lisane does."

M. Gustave nods. "But I own her."

"We don't have any coins at the moment—" Anneline begins.

Odette gives her a look that is sharp as a knife. "We'll bring the coins tomorrow," she tells M. Gustave.

"If you can't pay, I will have to kick you out," M. Gustave warns. He glances at Anneline. "Even if you're beautiful."

"We'll also want a bird on Thursday," Odette says to restore good feeling.

M. Gustave's feathered shoulders relax. He glances at Anneline and raises his thick eyebrows. "It will be plump. And juicy."

"Yes, yes," Anneline says wearily, removing her dirty gloves and falling back onto the mattress.

M. Gustave bows, then skulks through the door. A small storm of white and brown feathers eddies in his wake.

Four

As soon as M. Gustave is gone, Odette draws up a list in her mind of tasks and chores. Anneline arranges her filthy cape over her as a blanket. She waves a hand at Odette. "*Aline et Valcour.*"

Odette empties their velvet bag onto the uneven hearth and hands the novel, which she has mended numerous times, restitching the ragged spine, to her mother. Anneline sinks into its pages and is soon sighing and sucking her ring finger.

Anneline's fourth husband, the morose language teacher, had explained to Odette that *Aline et Valcour* was an "epistolary" novel: "From *epistle*, which means 'letter.' An epistolary novel is written as a series of letters between two characters. In this case the two are the fevered-with-love Aline and the wealthy Valcour."

"Could you read me some?" Odette had asked, curious.

The teacher had pinched his glasses onto his nose, mumbling, "You really must practice your reading." Then he had opened the book. "*You purify all that touches you. My senses are confused, reason leaves me. Why did I ever lay eyes on you? Why did your charming features intrude upon my soul...*"

"Enough!" Odette had shouted at the teacher. She had felt woozy and nauseous, as if she had eaten too many *puits d'amour* stuffed with vanilla cream and gooseberry jam. Odette didn't like desserts. She was an entrée person. She was not a dreamer; she was a doer.

"A bit rich, isn't it?" the teacher had agreed. "Well, the author sure is rich. He has sold many copies."

While Anneline sucks on her finger and sighs, Odette investigates their new home, breathing deeply from time to time to tamp down the excitement rising in her breast. She has moved too many times to be carried away with optimism. Still, she can't wait to dip a rag in soapy water, wring it—

the burbling music of industry—and scrub and scour, tidy and tame, and possibly turn a corner into a new life free of scuffs and humiliations.

Odette discovers a straw broom, missing only a few twigs, tucked beside the fireplace. She knows her way around repair. "Repair is next to godliness," Félix, her mother's third husband, had once sung as he repaired their wood floor with a piece of copper. He'd winked at Odette, showing off an eyelid dark with cemetery dirt. Félix spent his days as a gravedigger. The expression was really *cleanliness is next to godliness.* Even Odette, with an agnostic mother, knew that.

In addition to the broom, Odette finds a warped but serviceable wooden spoon, a hand spade, a sharpening stone and a battered tin pail. She holds the pail up to the window. Two spindles of light stream through. Not bad. The small holes will be easily repairable with a pinch of pitch mixed with pinesap.

The best discovery, though, is inside the armoire. Odette hears rustling, but she isn't afraid. She has met many mice and rats in her life. She pulls gently on the armoire door. As soon it is open a crack, a hen bursts out, screeching and flapping, black pinfeathers peppering the air.

"You must be Lisane," Odette says calmly. She grabs the anxious bird and holds her tight, squeezing her wings closed. "I'm sorry to disturb you. But I'm not a threat, I promise. Let me see what you're so protective of."

Lisane feebly pecks Odette's shoulder as Odette opens the armoire door wide. "I see."

A clutch of mottled brown eggs sits on a bed of twigs and cobwebs. As Lisane wriggles, Odette grazes the eggs' domed tops with her fingertips. The eggs are warm, which is a good sign. Odette sets the black hen on top of her silent brood. Lisane plops down protectively, fluffing her feathers the way cats puff their fur out double on cold days.

Odette closes the armoire door. Her head crowds with chores to be done. Firewood will be vital once the sun is down. A blanket too. Candles, rags, kettle and pot, lime and ash for soap, vegetables, meat, coins for rent. And corn and a dish for water so the black hen doesn't have to leave her burgeoning brood in the coming days. The bottoms of Odette's feet tickle, and her bones tingle.

It's the thrill of making do, the nimble calculations of resourcefulness.

The apartment's back door faces the front door. A leap across the meager hall could take a dog from one sill to the other. The back door opens onto a second flight of stone stairs, some of them worn so thin they seem to dribble into the next. The steps carry Odette down to a small yard walled in on all sides and tasseled in places with lemongrass and rosemary. A hoe nearly swallowed by brambles rests against a back wall.

Odette fetches her knife from the velvet bag and cuts willow stems to mend the broom. The folding knife was a gift for Anneline from Félix on their first—and only—anniversary. Odette was young at the time, but she remembers her mother peeling apples with the knife—they often picnicked in those days—and once Anneline had risked the blade's tip to pry open an oyster.

With the hoe, Odette clears the weeds around the rosemary and uncovers mint and wild carrots growing in the long grasses. As she makes room for them to flourish, the toe of her *sabot*, her wooden shoe, strikes something hard in the dirt. She digs and uncovers what looks like an enormous shinbone. She soon learns that it belonged to a horse, because at the narrow end of the shinbone lies a horseshoe. She reaches for the horseshoe and brushes off the dirt. It has hardly rusted. Good luck, indeed!

Odette surveys the ground. Lumps in the dirt sketch out the horse's entire skeleton. She determines where each shinbone comes to an end, the little mound where the hoof would be, and then digs.

M. Gustave had said that this house had been a guard's hut, so perhaps she has found the bones of a military horse, abandoned at the height of the chaos that was the Revolution. Odette knows that in the most fervent days, everyday tasks fell away. People forgot to eat. There was even a couple in her village who forgot their wedding day. It would not be impossible for a horse to be forgotten.

Odette uncovers all four horseshoes, as well as the twenty-four nails that once held them in place. The iron shoes, each stamped with a fleur-de-lis, have weight, and weight, Odette knows, is value. "I'll cover you up again later," Odette tells the forgotten horse. "I'm in a moment of need. Give me a night, and you will be at rest."

As she heads out of the yard, horseshoes jangling on her waist sash, she hears rock grind against rock. She turns as a shaft of light pierces the yard's east wall.

Odette's new house shares a wall with another, larger house. Odette had noticed it as they approached. The windows of the other house stood open, and duvets hung over the windowsills, airing. Odette thought she saw, inside one of the rooms, diapers strung up to dry. The yards, like the houses, share a wall. From which someone has now removed a stone.

Odette approaches the chink. When she is close enough, she swoops down and blazes her eye into the hole. Across the dark gap stares a dark eye with long lashes. It blinks, then pulls away.

Odette is enraged. "Are you a thief?" she calls. "Stealing a glimpse?" She takes a fistful of weeds and stuffs them into the hole. There is no sound from the other side. "I hear you breathing," Odette lies. She stands and puts her hands on her hips. "Sounds like you need to blow your nose." She studies the wall, takes in the places where the stones are not flush, maps a jagged path of toeholds and hand-holds, then springs.

In an instant she reaches the top.

At the same moment that he does.

Their faces are so close, the boy's breath curls up Odette's nose.

"What do you want?" she demands.

"To know who you are," the boy pants. "That's all. I'm sorry. No one has lived here since before I was born. Except for the black hen."

"Lisane."

"Niçois," the boy says. "Nice to meet you, Lisane."

"Lisane is the hen."

"Oh."

Niçois's hair is black and curly and down to his shoulders. His face is long, his nose too. His skin is nearly black. His eyes are gentle.

"At least could you tell me how to get to the baker's?" Odette asks.

"If you tell me your name," the boy counters. He swings himself up and sits astride the wall.

Odette remains silent.

Niçois gives up. "Fine. South until you meet the river, then east until you run into the cathedral, then northwest up the alley. People will be coming toward you with baguettes under their arms.

When people start moving away from you with baguettes under their arms, you're there."

"Clever," Odette says, dropping to the ground.

The boy's face falls. "I'm not. Come back up!"

Odette doesn't have time to sit on a wall, swinging her legs and chatting. "I can't."

"Then tell me your name."

Odette sighs. What can she do?

"Odette," she spits, and immediately feels lighter—as if she has been robbed.

Five

O dette hurries first to the blacksmith's. The man has dark hair, and his knuckles are lined with soot. He looks familiar, like a stranger she may have watched from a distance or someone in a dream. But, of course, she has never seen him before. She has never been to Nevers. He simply reminds her of other blacksmiths, she guesses, large with muscle and wet with sweat.

He turns the horseshoes over in his thick hands. "These are lovely. Beautifully made. I can melt them down," he says in a voice so deep Odette's *sabots* hum on her feet. "Who knows what they will become. Tool or weapon?"

The blacksmith drops several francs into Odette's hand. It's a good price. With the coins Odette buys a pot with only a few mends from a tinker, and a hunk of beef from the butcher. It would have been wiser to buy a cow's tongue, so much cheaper, but its texture—just softer than her own tongue—always makes her gag.

She scavenges an onion from the marketplace. It has been mildly crushed, by a cartwheel, likely, or a hoof, the skin cracked and its layers exposed, but after a rinse in the city's wide river, it will be fine to eat—perhaps even more flavorful, Odette thinks, than an onion that has experienced nothing. That's the kind of thing Félix would have said.

Finally Odette stands at the bakery's back door with one of her *sabots* in her hand, lined with dirt so it won't catch fire. She coughs to get the attention of the baker's helper, a boy with an uneven thatch of wheat-blond hair who, without a word, shovels up embers from the bread oven and tips them in.

As Odette hobbles on one *sabot* down the lane toward her new home, a large, well-dressed man follows after her. "Miss!" he calls. "May I smell your hands?" It is the man who giggled when the piglet sniffed at Anneline's ankles.

Odette is shocked. "My hands? No!"

"Just a sniff. To identify where you are from, since it's clear you aren't from here. Those shoes, that tunic—"

"No."

"I am a scientist. A professor. I study hand smells. At the Sorbonne."

"The Sorbonne?" Anneline always boasts that her first husband studied at the Sorbonne.

"Well, I *was* a professor."

"Maybe one day," Odette says doubtfully. She gestures at the ashes smoking in her shoe. "I'm in a hurry."

The professor wishes her well and bows low. Odette hears him sniff as his nose passes near her hands.

She is nearly giddy as she flies home. She has food for supper, a cooking pot, embers to start a fire and enough coins left over from selling the horseshoes to pay M. Gustave the first moon's rent. Mother will be proud, she thinks.

No. Anneline is never proud—only tired or bored, unless she is blissfully in love. Odette finds her still curled up under her cloak on the sad mattress.

"Is that you?" Anneline asks weakly. "I'm so cold."

"I'm starting a fire. I'll make a beef stew with carrot root, onion and mint."

"Good. I'm ravenous."

But Anneline starts to snore just as Odette gets the fire crackling. Odette shakes her when the stew is ready, but Anneline doesn't waken. Her mother is very warm, Odette notes. Perspiring.

Anneline sleeps through the entire afternoon, while Odette fills gaps in the house's stone walls with a paste of mud and grass. Anneline snores through the evening, while Odette sweeps the floors and replaces the missing windowpanes with roof slates she finds in the street. Anneline doesn't even wake as Odette removes the rotting straw from the mattress beneath her to cram in fresh, new grass, which she has cut from the yard with the folding knife.

As she always does when she holds the knife's smooth olive-wood handle in her hand, she had thought of Félix. He had taught her how to sharpen it. "It mustn't reflect a speck of light," he had said, holding the sharp blade toward the sunlight. "But don't get carried away: every time you sharpen a knife, you lose a bit of it. You could sharpen it to nothing." He'd then held the knife over his black hat so she could watch the dust of the blade's steel fall like fine silver rain.

After Félix died Odette claimed the knife for herself. Whenever she produces it, Anneline turns her head sharply. Félix was not like her mother's other husbands.

Of the deaths Anneline has inadvertently caused, five were those of her own spouses. The deaths hardly affected her though. She adjusted each time by adopting a small, eccentric habit. When the teacher died, she stopped eating raspberries. Ever since the bank manager died, she stomps when a robin comes near. And ever since the mill owner succumbed, she butters her bread heavily. When Odette's librarian father died, Anneline stopped wearing panniers, she told Odette—which actually made sense.

The two had been married only one month. By the time Odette was born, the pale, long-faced, drop-of-royal-blood librarian had been crushed under the wheels of a horse cart. He had been holding Anneline's hand, helping her hop across a puddle, but as she leaped she knocked him into the street. "My Paris panniers," she'd explained to Odette.

There persists a foolish affectation among women who, to be fashionable, strap baskets to their hips before putting on their dresses. The panniers make their hips appear impossibly wide—sometimes as wide as a harpsichord. Women often have to turn sideways to get through a door. To me the fashion is inexplicable. Are women boasting that they can afford the silk required to cover these exaggerated hips? Are they hoping to lure men, indicating that they will surely birth healthy children, having so much room to incubate them? Sometimes I wonder, with all the burdens on them, do women simply want more space? Whatever the reason, the silly fashion killed the librarian who was responsible for Odette's elongated nose and sizable ears.

But while the death of the father of her only child had hardly affected Anneline, Félix's death nearly undid her.

Félix's love had been solid, earthy and hearty. When he died Anneline forgot the language of her true self, which Félix, who through his work understood life better than most, had kindled. His love had revealed the spritely girl with laughing intelligence and easy depths that Anneline had been before she was plunked in a convent school run by cruel nuns. With Félix, Anneline had been happy. Filled to the brim. This had made her generous. For the first time, Odette had been able to be a child.

Odette was only five when Félix and her mother married, but she remembers him perfectly. The memories are immediate and as deep as dreams. Odette remembers the boom of his laugh—a laugh, her mother once said, that could make flowers bloom. He could be serious though. Thoughtful.

Odette had often kept Félix company as he dug fresh graves in the cemetery. Her mother liked her out of the house, and Félix was happy to have her near. Odette felt warm when she was with him, when he made her a grass doll or talked to her about the lives of the dead or lifted her onto his shoulders for the walk home, singing "*à la claire fontaine, m'en allant promener.*" At those times she had felt that of all the places in the world, she was in the right one.

When she calls Félix to mind, she sees the worn toes of his boots and hears his shovel—*schlunk*—sliding into the earth. She remembers the dirt that filled the wrinkles of his knuckles and the thick yellow rivers that flowed from his nostrils until he wiped them on the back of his sleeve. Anneline's husbands before and after Félix were calm men who took pride in being respectable. Félix was not interested in respectability, and he was suspicious of pride.

When Félix spoke the words dropped from his lips as sure as fishing weights. It seems to Odette that everything Félix ever said has stayed with her, that his memory is bound up with hers. Perhaps that is the nature of grieving someone so large and alive. Their life burrows into yours. How else can you say goodbye?

Once, Félix had reached into a grave, then straightened and perched two small skulls on Odette's shoulders. They were children's skulls that he had dug up by accident. "A couple of playmates for you," he had said. "I will have to bury them again, but why don't you give them an afternoon in the sun?"

Odette had played for hours with the skulls. She'd danced with them in the shade of the lime trees and, during a short rain, cowered with them in the hollow of a tulip tree's trunk. She'd propped them on a gravestone and given them a lesson in counting. As she counted "one, two..." a pair of yellow-rumped warblers had flown down and perched one on each skull. They had begun to sing there, to trill, and a shiver went through Odette. She imagined that the birds were the children's souls, returned to earth.

With Félix, Anneline had breathed deeply. She'd scratched her mosquito bites vigorously. She'd eaten with gusto, her hands pressed close to her lips. Her voice had been full and resonant. In those days she'd squat to stir the fire. She'd draw Odette between her legs, give her the poker and teach her how to make sparks fly and coals throb. But ever since Félix died, nearly ten years ago, her mother's voice has been as light as gauze, vulnerable to any wind, each word a fleck of ash.

One morning about nine years ago, while Odette and Félix were in the graveyard, Anneline plucked a chicken, stuffed it with turnips and roasted it over a fire, which she—*she*, who had not started a fire in years—had raised expertly from a single ember. Roast chicken stuffed with turnips was Félix's favorite repast. Anneline carried the meal to the graveyard in a basket along with bread, cheese and

Hungarian wine, and she and Félix perched side by side on a gravestone to consume their feast, Odette skipping around them as they talked.

In the middle of their conversation, Félix went silent.

He fell to his knees, then crawled to Anneline and wrapped his arms around her waist. His face was blue.

Anneline screamed. "What is it? What are you doing?"

And then, his head on Anneline's lap and a hand reaching toward Odette, Félix died. He had choked on a bone from the roast chicken.

In the days that followed Anneline cried until the trails where her tears ran down her cheeks scabbed over.

She left no room for Odette to cry too.

Now, when the moon is high and gleaming like a freshly sharpened scythe, Odette lies down next to her mother and falls into a sleep that she has earned with every muscle and hair. Her mother is still very warm. She seems to have a terrible fever.

Six

A magnificent croak cracks the night open, startling Odette from her sleep.

The croak sounds again. Something needs oiling, Odette thinks.

She leans out the window and listens. She is sure it is a donkey, braying with surprising earnestness.

"*Chut!* That's enough!" someone yells from a window down the road.

"Silence, you noisy donkey!" shouts another.

"You will be all right," calls a third more gently. "All will soon be well."

But the donkey continues its hoarse cries. It is trying to tell us something, Odette thinks, remembering a small dog that had once persistently nipped at her apron until she noticed the shard of blue glass lodged in its leathery paw. Odette had dislodged the piece of glass, using the tip of Félix's knife, and the dog bounded off, barking twice. Another time, while braiding Anneline's hair, Odette had been vexed by distant high-pitched whimpering. She had followed the sound and discovered a mouse struggling to stay afloat in a well. This mouse also Odette rescued.

Odette can hear the townspeople violently slamming their shutters against the donkey's voice. Should she join the others of Nevers, as heartless as they seem, and return to sleep?

She listens closely for a few more moments. Perhaps the dear animal has a toothache or a hoof swollen from laminitis.

Hi han. Hi han.

Well, all donkeys can sound as though they're in pain, Odette reflects.

But then, incredibly, she understands what the donkey is saying. The donkey is braying in Latin. Odette is sure of it. *Vos, in lectis vestris!* she hears. The wide forehead of Anneline's fourth husband, Victor, the polyglot, comes to mind, with his thin lips and bad breath, scolding Odette when she grumbled about his lessons: "Latin is a wellspring. There is no French without it. Honor your roots, child!"

Odette listens intently to the donkey's congested whinnies, teasing out the words. "You in your soft beds!" it shouts. It then goes on: "Asleep and dreaming. Be glad that you do not stand ankle deep in mud at odds with the horizon. Be grateful that you are not a donkey."

Odette's ears labor. *Stellae aequo frigido animo spectant.* "The stars stare with icy indifference. The moon is a silent howl. Insects scuttle. Rats leap."

Finally, energy waning, the donkey repeats, *Cupio asinus non esse.* "I wish I were not a donkey. I wish I were not a donkey. I wish I were not a donkey." At last, silence returns.

When Odette wakes in the morning, with not even the hem of Anneline's cloak over her— Anneline has taken it all for herself—she decides she must have dreamed the donkey. Donkeys don't speak. Not in French. Certainly not in Latin.

On the other hand, Odette has never once been fooled by a dream.

She rises and blows on the coals in the fireplace, planning to make some tea and porridge.

Anneline stirs. She stretches and yawns. Then she freezes, horrified. "Did I have a baby last night?"

"Of course not," Odette answers.

Anneline gestures toward her feet. "Look!"

Odette's eyes trace the outlines of her mother's legs under the cloak and then, between them, a surprising third lump. The lump moves. It thrusts.

"I've always been careful," Anneline cries, her eyes wild. "After you, I mean. A sponge dipped in vinegar works. Animal intestines are handy too—you tie one end and pull it over like a sock. Of course, simply separating at the right time, just before the big excitement—"

"Mother!"

The lump tosses and twists under the cloak. "Well, if it's a boy he will have to share your inheritance. Thanks to the revolutionaries, daughters matter as much as boys. In the old days you would have gotten nothing."

"You have nothing to leave, Mother."

"There's still time. I'm not going to die tomorrow." Anneline pats her chin. "Does my neck sag so you think I'm at death's door?"

The lump between Anneline's legs snorts. Odette yanks the cloak away and there, snout gleaming, wriggles the freckled piglet.

"Oh!" Anneline says and sighs.

Odette eyes the front door. When she latched it the night before, she had doubted the keeper, which was wobbly on its nails. Sure enough, it now lies on the floor. The excited piglet must have pushed on the door and knocked the keeper loose, gaining entry.

With another snort the little animal bounces off the bed, trots to the armoire and sniffs at the cupboard's crooked door.

"Eggs," Odette tells Anneline. "About to hatch. Oh no!"

In a flash the piglet has nosed open the armoire door and leaped inside. Lisane, surprised, squawks and flaps her wings frantically in the small space, knocking an egg to the floor.

Odette hurries over and cradles the egg in her hands. It has a single fine crack. The piglet leaps excitedly around Odette as if the egg were his. His little snout knocks the egg from her hand. This time it hits the floor with a crunch, and a damp clump of yellow feathers rolls out. Before Odette can retrieve the helpless chick, the piglet starts to lick it. Lisane, still flapping about, stabs at the piglet with her beak, but the piglet continues to lick the yellow ball. *Slurp, snuff, snort.* It is single-minded. Nothing in all the universe is more important.

The chick begins to move. Its thin legs tremble and stretch. Its little shoulders shrug, and finally its dewy eyes open. The chick stares at the piglet, who calmly stares back. They keep their round black eyes on each other.

"This chick is quite big," Odette calls to Anneline. "The others can't be far behind."

"How many others?"

"Five. Once they're grown and laying, roosters aside, we'll have all the eggs we want."

"Well"—Anneline smooths the cloak over her legs—"at least I haven't had another baby. One slows you down enough."

Odette long ago devised a way to stop her mother's thoughtless words from piercing her heart

—she imagines a Gaul warrior's breastplate where her ribs are.

"I suffered last night," Anneline says. "But I'm better now. Even the bed seems softer than it was." She stands and pulls her cloak tightly around her. "Do you have a coin so I can get some paper? I must post my notice."

"You shouldn't go out," Odette says. "You were fevered in the night."

"New town, new hope," Anneline recites. She runs her fingers through her hair and re-pins her chignon. "I have a good feeling."

"You always do," Odette says.

"This time I really do."

"You always *really do.*"

"Well, this time I really, really do."

Every time they land somewhere new, Anneline posts a note in the town square.

Five summers ago, the year that Robespierre was guillotined, you arranged delivery of a small package marked "for A and child" to Madame Lamont's boarding house in Cluny. It held a key and directions to a bridge where

*a wooden box was wedged between the girders.
The key worked, but the box was empty. I am
sorry to have failed you. Contact me at…*

No one has ever responded. But Anneline persists.

The letter that came with the key said the contents of the box wedged under the bridge would unite Anneline with her "dead husband's wealthy family."

Anneline had a few dead husbands from wealthy families—families she knew had no wish to be reunited with her, considering her culpability in the men's deaths. Still, she was curious. The merest hint of wealth stirs curiosity in people, I have noticed. They stop talking incessantly about themselves and start asking question after question. It is as if they hope to ferret out a secret path or some potion that will secure riches for themselves.

Odette thinks there is something more than greed that drives her mother to keep searching though. She thinks that Anneline hopes the box somehow concerns Félix. Félix had lost touch with his only sibling during the Revolution, which aggrieved him.

Perhaps this brother has fallen into riches and wants to share them with her.

Anneline has no siblings. Her mother died in childbirth, and her father followed soon after, dead of a broken heart. So Anneline was delivered to a Catholic orphanage when she was three.

"We didn't even have our own beds," she told Odette one night after she had had too much wine. "We were moved every night."

Odette is grateful sometimes when her mother drinks too much wine. It opens her like a book, and her memories pour onto her tongue. "They didn't want us to get attached to anything or anyone. If we did, we might unite and defy the nuns. If two of us laughed together, we were separated. Some of us developed ways of laughing that didn't look like laughing. Hopping on one foot, for example, or tugging an earlobe. Trust me though—we cried far more than we laughed."

So when Anneline received a package with a key and a note mentioning wealth and family, she had been intrigued. Odette, though only nine, had found a farmer willing to rent out his rowboat and had rowed her mother down the Saône until they reached the bridge. As soon as they spied the box wedged between its beams, Anneline had leaped up, upsetting the boat. Odette, trying to restore balance, fell into the cold, murky river.

The box was empty except for a scrawled note. It read:

I got here first!

Soggy and dispirited, Anneline and Odette hadn't spoken the entire way home. Odette rowed and Anneline sobbed. Silently. Chest heaving. Shoulders shaking, tears digging gullies through her face powder. Her quiet sobbing had struck Odette. Normally when Anneline cried, she made ample noise, her sobs demands for attention, for favors. Odette realized in this moment of Anneline sobbing quietly with a kind of purity that her mother had wishes Odette had never imagined.

"Why are you crying, Mother?" she had asked softly.

"I-I—" Anneline blotted the streams of kohl pencil beneath her eyes with the backs of her index fingers. "I wanted some independence.

That is all. Let's not speak of it again." Anneline shook her long, shining hair and looked over the boat's edge. "If Félix were here, he would bash one of those fish with the back of an oar. He would tear out the backbone and vertebrae as a tailor would stitching. And we would feast."

Odette had itched to bash one of the pale bodies that swarmed around them, but she knew it would rock the boat dangerously again, which her mother would not appreciate. Three nights later, however, she wove a trap from reeds and left it in the river for an hour. But when she presented her prey to her mother, Anneline stared at it blankly. "A dead fish? Really, Odette."

Now, in Nevers, Odette hands her mother a coin for her to buy some paper. Her mother doesn't ask where the coins came from. She never does. Visibly shivering, Anneline steps into her satin shoes. The shoes are pink, embroidered with silver thread, perhaps the most beautiful item she owns, but the color is fading, and the toes are frayed.

"Do you have to put up the notice?" Odette asks. "No one ever responds. And we need the coins to pay M. Gustave. And buy a chicken from him. You promised him."

"Of course I need to post the notice," Anneline answers. "You'll see. Someone will answer one day. You, girl, need to learn about persistence."

Seven

The chicks tap steadily at their shells. Odette pours water into a piece of a pottery jug she found in the yard and picks nasturtiums to add to the corn, so that Lisane can stay near her chicks while they hatch, a high-pitched parade that could take three days. Meanwhile, the spotted piglet carries its beloved chick gently in its jaws and sets it near the fire, then lies down and curls around it.

Odette firmly secures the keeper to the door, then returns to the yard to start a garden bed. While digging, she feels in her shoulder blades a humming alertness, a self-awareness that makes it difficult to concentrate on her work.

"I see you," she says.

"You can't possibly see me. Unless you have eyes in the back of your head."

"Then *you* see *me*. I know you are watching me."

"Meet me up top," Niçois begs through the chink in the wall.

"I'm busy."

"You're shy."

"That's presumptuous."

"I don't know what that means."

"It means you think you know things before you actually do."

"I don't know anything."

"That's impossible."

Niçois scrambles up the wall. "Come up. It's fun."

Odette continues to dig.

Sitting on top of the wall, Niçois swings his feet and whistles as he peels bark from a stick. His frivolousness makes Odette work harder at clearing the ground. She gathers fallen branches to map out a hexagonal shape for the small plot.

"That's pretty," Niçois says. He lies along the top of the wall and crosses his hands over his belly. White moths flit around him. He closes his eyes. "Where are you from?" he asks sleepily.

"Places," Odette grunts. "Lots of places."

"I was born in this town. In Nevers. I learned to crawl here, to walk here, to run here. I know every corner. As my mother likes to say, my ears have heard every church bell that has rung in the past thirteen years, and every clap of thunder."

Odette thrusts her hoe into the ground.

Niçois continues. "I have consumed only water from its wells, and bread made from the wheat of its fields. I am made of this place. Made of here."

Odette clenches her jaw. Would he ever be quiet?

She is made of tumult. The only steady thing in her life is her unsteady mother. It is very important for Odette to get the six edges of the garden straight and sure. And to keep digging. To keep working.

But life was tumult for everyone, wasn't it? Always changing, whether they realized it or not. Every bell Niçois heard had rung differently— the clapper striking in new places—at a different hour on a different day, hadn't it? Way back when Odette was small and hopeful, Félix had once told her, as he stood waist deep in a new grave, "You can never step into the same river twice."

Odette had sat at the edge of the grave, her chubby legs swinging in the dark, cool air, heels brushing against the new grave's side, loosening sprays of soil. "Or the same grave," she had answered, smiling.

Félix laughed heartily. "That is true. I have been hopping in and out of this one all day, and each time I do, it's a little deeper."

"You're like a gopher," the young Odette said.

The gravedigger reached out and tousled her hair, peppering her scalp with crumbs of dirt. He grew serious. "I guess everything stops when you're dead. The same forever."

"Don't ever die," Odette whispered.

"I'll do my best," Félix had said. "For you."

Odette plunges her garden spade into the dirt.

On top of the wall, Niçois yawns. "When you close your eyes, do you see church windows?"

Odette knows just what he means. "No," she answers.

"Pieces of colored glass, shimmering. Or sunlight on the back of a river."

"No," Odette repeats. She stands and stretches. She watches the piglet as it trots out the back door, hops down the top two steps, then turns around and squeals. The chick, already on its feet, wobbles after it and peeps. The piglet squeals encouragingly. The chick edges toward the stairs, then tumbles and rolls. The piglet leaps down the next two steps and this time guides the chick with its snout. They continue this way, with the piglet squealing and snuffling and the chick peeping, until they reach the yard.

"I wonder if we sound like that to them," Niçois says.

Odette laughs despite herself.

"Peep," Niçois says.

"Snort," Odette replies, and then she flushes. She sizes up the hexagonal patch of dirt.

"You need a pitchfork," Niçois says, leaping off the wall and out of sight into his own yard. A minute later he arrives at the top of the wall again, panting a little. "Stand back!"

Odette steps back, and Niçois hurls the pitchfork so that its teeth sink into the hexagon of bare earth. Then, its grip not deep enough, the pitchfork falls over.

Niçois leaps down so that Odette and he stand face-to-face. They are of identical height.

"How old are you?" Niçois asks.

"Fourteen."

Niçois smiles. Something thrums in Odette, a slow lightning bolt, warming her from the top of her head to the tips of her toes.

"My mother says that work is best accomplished if you take regular periods of rest," Niçois says. "When a woman gives birth, she's wracked with pains for a minute or two. And then she gets to rest between them for several minutes. Contractions, they're called. The seizing pain."

Odette wonders how this boy knows more about childbirth than she does.

"Well, I can't rest. There's no time." She doesn't like how her voice sounds. She draws her lips between her teeth and gnaws them to get them to soften. "I did need a pitchfork," she says, prying up a block of dirt and flipping it over. "Thank you."

The chick totters over to Niçois. The boy takes a chunk of Odette's freshly turned soil and holds it near the chick, pointing at the beetles scurrying across it, and making kissing noises with his lips. The chick clicks her beak, then clamps onto a bug and gobbles it down. Then another. She eats until her eyes shrink and she collapses into sleep. The piglet carries her gently between his teeth to a shady spot and lies beside her, kicking away any fly or ant that comes close.

Odette wipes her face with her apron. She surveys her work.

"My mother has seeds," Niçois says. "Mostly for herbs, but vegetables too."

Something loosens in Odette. The spacious feeling is unfamiliar—frightening and pleasant at once. She takes a deep breath of the earthy air and feels she has not breathed so deeply in a long time.

"I heard something very strange last night," she tells Niçois. "A donkey, I think."

Niçois laughs. "You and everyone else. That was Anne. He doesn't mean to wake us all up. He can't help himself."

"Clever name for a donkey," Odette says (since *âne* means "donkey.") "Though it is a female's name."

"It just seems to fit. People have tried others. The Great Disruptor was one. But really, he's softhearted."

Odette considers telling Niçois about understanding Anne's brays. But he would think she was silly, which she isn't. She must just have been tired, she tells herself.

Niçois's eyes light up. "You must meet him! He stands in a small field in the shadow of the cathedral. Let me show you. I'll show you all of Nevers! Its roads and alleys, the paths to the river, the *faïence* factories—they're closed up now, nothing but piles of broken pottery. Let me show you why Nevers is the best town in the world."

"How would you know?" Odette laughs. "You've never been to any other."

"It must be the best town in the world," Niçois says, "because I am perfectly happy here."

Odette looks at him doubtfully.

He smiles. "You will be too."

"You don't know that."

Niçois looks down at his feet. "Presumptuous."

Odette thrusts the pitchfork into the dirt so that it stays. "Show me."

Eight

To a bird in the sky, the town of Nevers is a handful of stones flung on a grassy slope facing the slow, wide Loire River. Poor people, who can't afford land in town, build houses on the other side of the river, which floods in spring when the river rises. If there is one thing I have learned, it is that the poor have fewer choices than the wealthy. Poverty is like a prison or a bad spell that is nearly impossible to break.

Niçois leads Odette to a green expanse beside the river. They watch boatmen moving coal from one boat to another. On the river's edge, not far away, a crowd of women wash mountains of clothes. The air reverberates with the spanks of their paddles.

"My mother is down there with all five of my shirts," Niçois tells Odette as a yellow butterfly alights on his head. "Well, except this one that I'm wearing. The women of Nevers wash the family clothes twice a year. It takes three days. They call the first day Purgatory—you know, where people wait after dying to see whether they've made it into heaven or not? That was yesterday. The clothes were boiled in water and ash and left to soak overnight.

"This morning the laundry cart rolled through the town's streets. Women load their wet laundry onto the cart, then climb on top and bump down to the river. Sometimes they sing. Perhaps you heard them?"

Odette had. She had wondered drowsily if it was a traveling band that would be singing for coins in the marketplace.

"Today the work is hard, as you can see," Niçois says. Odette watches the women, their backs bent over rocks, kneading and slapping their clothes incessantly. "Their arms will ache for weeks. Today is Hell.

"But tomorrow, when the clothes are clean and dry and have the smell of green air and crisp sunshine—tomorrow is Paradise."

Green air and crisp sunshine, Odette thinks to herself. She knows those smells but would never have found words for them. Niçois uses words in ways she has never heard.

Two women gather up the washed pants and shirts and jackets and twist them until no more water squeezes out. Then they lay the clothing across the tall grass to dry. The side of the hill is covered.

"For a few *sous*, older boys watch over the clothes at night," Niçois explains. "The women used to just leave the clothes unattended. But sometimes river birds would walk across them, leaving wayward tracks, or martens would chew on the ties, and once a fox got its head stuck in the sleeve of a white sleeping gown."

Odette laughs.

"He zigzagged though town, frantic. He was like a shooting star that had touched down on earth. A couple of women cornered him in the cemetery and cut him free. He ran off with his tail between his legs."

Niçois looks at the river and shudders. He tells Odette the story learned by every child in Nevers. When the Roman empire blanketed France,

Caesar kept the empire's treasury and food supply in Nevers, in a camp by the Loire. The ancient Celtic people of the area, the Aedui, attacked the camp, taking all the treasure and as much of the Romans' stores of corn as they could. What corn they couldn't take they burned or dumped into the Loire.

Odette tries to imagine it—men yelling in pain, blood washing down the banks and swirling pink when it meets the river, fires crackling, the sweet smell of corn.

But the chatter and splashing of the women dissolve her visions to nothing. They talk vigorously, often exploding into what sounds like naughty giggles.

"Hell or not," Odette says, "they're having fun."

"Yes," Niçois agrees. "My mother likes to complain about washing day, but she comes home excited with lots to tell."

Children play around the women. Every so often one is scolded for splashing mud on a clean shirt or going too near the river. One child gets a wet cloth across her face—a sobering punishment that makes Odette wince. For all her faults, Anneline has never touched Odette in anger.

"What is your mother like?" she asks Niçois. "Would she ever slap you with a wet cloth?"

Niçois stretches back onto the grass. "She's the mother of mothers," he says. A second yellow butterfly has joined the first atop his hair. They perch there trustingly, as if Niçois were some kind of plant. "She has hundreds of children."

"Impossible!" Odette says. "A woman in the Jura, where I once lived, had twenty-eight babies. But I've never heard of someone having *hundreds*."

Niçois smiles. "My mother is a midwife, the only one in Nevers. I have sometimes been her assistant. She chases the husbands out of the houses, sends them on silly errands, then coos to the women, *You are doing fine. I can feel the head. A hairy one, this one. Turn onto your heart side.*

"Then suddenly she'll shout, *PUSH! PUSH! PUSH!* and out comes the newest citizen of Nevers, squalling. My mother wraps the baby in a length of new hemp, puts her finger in its mouth and, once it starts to suck, declares, *This is a strong one.* She's good, my mother. Warm. And cold when she needs to be."

"Why would she need to be cold?"

"When she has to take action. When the baby's too quiet, because the navel string is wrapped around its neck. Or sometimes the baby wants to come out legs first. Sometimes the mother gets a terrible fever afterward, and those are the saddest days. Sometimes mothers die."

Niçois's eyes cloud over. Then he brightens. "But usually not. She has the best reputation. Another midwife tried to open shop in Nevers, but everyone wants my mother. She is already delivering the babies of the babies she guided into the world."

"So she's a grandmother." Odette smiles.

"I guess! Which makes me an uncle." Niçois laughs. The butterflies lift off, flit about in the air, then land again on his head. He doesn't seem to notice them.

"And you have many, many siblings."

"Well, yes. But no. None. My mother had no other children. There are few like me—people with no brothers or sisters."

"I am like you," Odette says.

Niçois looks up at her and grins. The lightning warms her from head to toe again.

"Now, to answer your question, my mother would never hit me with a wet cloth. But my father might have. Once, when I left the gate open and the goats got out, guess what he did?"

"What?"

"Pulled down my pants and spanked me—with nettles!"

Odette laughs.

"I haven't been naughty since."

Niçois unplugs a dandelion from the ground and chews on its pale root.

Odette lies back on the grass alongside him. She is surprised by her ease. The sky above is blue for as far as she can see.

But she has a lot to do today. She sits up and looks around. Out on the river two muscled fishermen haul a full net of wriggling fish out of the water and into their boat.

Then Odette's heart squirms. Not far away at all, half hidden behind the wrinkled trunk of an acacia tree, a small man with straight, yellow hair is watching her through a spyglass. As soon as Odette sees him, he ducks out of sight.

Nine

Odette gathers the courage to look toward the tree again, but the man is gone. She wonders if perhaps she only imagined him there, if her mind played tricks with the tree's shadow. But she's unsettled. She stands and nudges Niçois with the toe of her *sabot.* "Show me more of your favorite town."

Niçois opens his eyes. "The factories first. You said you needed dishes. Then I'll show you the mill and then introduce you to Anne, the noisy donkey."

Niçois and Odette walk along the river until they reach the Pont de Loire, a long bridge that halfway across the river, strangely, turns from stone to wood. Niçois explains that a flood nine years earlier washed five of the bridge's stone arches into the river.

Once across the bridge, they arrive at an abandoned factory. The hand-painted *faïence* bowls, plates, cups, tureens, busts and inkwells Nevers is famous for were once baked in great kilns there, Niçois says. Blackbirds flap in and out through broken windows, and shattered pottery litters the floor. Odette and Niçois dig through the piles and find two bowls and two cups, mostly intact, that are decorated with blue flowers.

Then Odette finds a plate with neither a crack nor a chip. On the front is painted a girl, standing in a street and holding a small basket.

"She looks like you!" Niçois exclaims. "With the same brown hair and serious face."

Odette knows she is a serious girl—her mother has often teased her about it unkindly. But the way Niçois says it is kind. Without judgment.

She studies the plate again. The girl is her age and wears wooden shoes and a similar apron and dress. She stands in front of an arch Odette saw on their first day wandering through town. But the girl on the plate looks stronger. More sure. Less lost.

"I will need a basket like that when Lisane's chicks start laying eggs," Odette muses aloud. "For selling door to door." Her voice softens. "Until then I don't know how I'll earn any *sous*."

Niçois shrugs. "That's easy. Mother always says she doesn't have enough hands as a midwife. I can only help so much. I'll talk to her."

The idea both thrills and frightens Odette. Once, in Sigy-le-Châtel, Odette had come upon a distressed nanny goat. Her newborn kid lay motionless in the grass. Odette, who had once heard farmers speak of "swinging a kid," first spoke gently to the new mother, then gripped the baby's back hooves and swung it gently in a circle. The kid choked up fluid and took its first breath. Odette was elated for days. After that the kid always licked her hand when she was near.

But human babies? She looks at Niçois.

He smiles as if he knows just what she's thinking. "You'll learn quickly."

Odette and Niçois peer out a factory window at the scene below. Niçois produces a heel of bread from his pocket and tears it in two for them to share.

"What about your father?" Odette asks. "What does he do?"

"My father is dead."

"Oh!"

"As a boy, he fished with his mother and father, but when he got older he got his own boat and delivered *faïence* destined for Paris. My father was an excellent boatman, famous for having never delivered a broken piece. Not one. The Loire's waters get rough, but he seemed to know its every gurgle and burp." Niçois pointed across the river. "Do you see that pile of rubble? That's the hut he grew up in. He said there were so many gaps between the stones that during storms the house whistled like someone playing the clavichord."

Odette laughs.

"He was funny. He cleaned his ears with twigs, danced right up on the supper table when he was happy. He'd weep when my mother told him about babies that didn't make it, how she had had to close their eyes, their life no more than a blink. He believed in the Revolution. And that's what did him in."

"But the Revolution was for people just like him."

"Yes. And he embraced it. He organized. He was taught by Chaumette."

Odette gasps. "Pierre Gaspard Chaumette? The great revolutionary? My mother sobbed the day he was beheaded, and ate an entire baguette, dipping each hunk in cream. I swear her tears turned white from all the milk."

"Chaumette was born here in Nevers. He changed his name, you know. Pierre was too Christian for him."

"He didn't believe," Odette says.

"He believed in equality. But the church believes some people are closer to God than others. I've seen a lot of babies," Niçois says. "Every one is born naked, wailing and amazed. Equal."

"Anaxagoras!" Odette exclaims suddenly. "That's the name my mother sighed between bites of her baguette."

"That's the name Pierre Chaumette took, yes."

"My mother's husband thought she was mooning for Chaumette, that she was in love with Chaumette, but…"

"What?"

Odette falls silent. She can't believe how much she's talking. What she is thinking is that her mother's sympathy for Chaumette was really for herself. Chaumette was a simple cobbler's son who had risen in the world to become a surgeon and then a leader of the Revolution, fighting for the lowly.

Anneline had been a lowly little girl in an orphanage, counting her hungry ribs at night, crying herself to sleep only to be scolded by the crow-like nuns for keeping the other children awake. Chaumette had been that girl's champion.

"The original Anaxagoras was a Greek thinker," she says instead. Her mother's fourth husband, Victor, had told her this. "He believed the world is made up of tiny things that never change. Everything in the world—including us!—is made of two or more of these tiny ingredients. Everything is a mixture. A recipe. But, he said, *Each one is… most manifestly those things of which there are the most in it.*"

Odette has chewed over those words many times. She plays a game with herself, guessing the main ingredient of the things around her. Some are easy. Bread is mostly wheat, clothing is mostly hemp or flax, a pot is mostly iron, a candle mostly wax. But what about *her*? What is she mostly made of? She and her mother had eaten a lot of potatoes when her mother was been between marriages. So perhaps that. But they had also eaten well during some marriages, so perhaps lamb and gooseberry pie.

When she was with Félix, she'd been made of something other than food. Something that filled her heart the way sunshine warms the body.

"Anaxagoras said each of us has an unseen apparatus in us. *Nous*, he called it. The organ for thinking and remembering."

Niçois taps his forehead. "Our minds."

"Exactly."

"I don't have the best one. Mother says I'm all heart."

Sometimes Odette's mind is so full it seems to be all of what she is. It's filled with memories and chunks of knowledge people have shared with her, cooking directions, bills to be settled, items needing mending, chores to be done. So many chores. That's it. Odette is made of chores. Work is her chief ingredient.

Odette glances at Niçois. He is gazing foggily across the river as an ant ambles along a seam of his shirt, dragging a dropped crumb of bread. This boy is *not* made of work, Odette thinks. What is he made of? Laziness? *Light*, her mind answers.

Niçois turns to face her. "My father fell under Chaumette's charm. He started to give speeches and organize protests in the streets. *Share the land!*

Everyone is equal. No rich, no poor. All are free to chart their destiny. He spent all of our money on torches and paper and ink and—weapons. He gave the Revolution a home in Nevers. Robespierre spent a night at our house."

Odette can't believe it. "*The-king-must-die-so-the-country-can-live* Robespierre? *Terror-is-justice* Robespierre? *Pity-is-treason* Robespierre?"

"That Robespierre, yes. He came to rouse us with speeches."

"Robespierre was in Nevers?"

"He slept in my bed."

"Can I see your bed?" Odette claps a hand over her mouth. *What a thing to ask!*

"Of course." Niçois smiles happily. "You should have seen the crowds when he was here. People came from fifty miles away, traveling farther than they had ever traveled in their lives.

"My father was the first to speak. He told the people of Nevers that they worked hard in the sun and rain to feed the people of France. They made the plates the wealthy ate from. They worked harder than the rich, he said, and what did they have to show for it? Shoes with holes. Children swollen with hunger.

Pennies wrapped in a kerchief at the back of a drawer. While the wealthy in Paris danced under chandeliers and gorged themselves on finger foods!

"*Do you have pocket watches*? he asked. *Do you have silk handkerchiefs? Baths and bidets and tailored suits? No! But you build this country from earth and seed.* You *are the true children of France.*"

"It worked," Odette says.

"Sure. People rose up. They fought the rich with knives and the guillotine." Niçois looks suddenly weary, windblown. "It was an exciting time, but it was horrible too. In the big cities blood flowed in the streets, fast as rainwater. Nevers was calmer, but at times my mother kept me in the house for days on end. I was not allowed to look out the window."

Odette has always been grateful that during the bloodiest months of the Revolution, she and her mother lived in a small village. She was seven at the time, and Anneline left Odette alone to travel briefly to Lyon to see things for herself. She came home wild with pride and fury and fear.

"If I prick my finger on a thorn, my mother hardly glances at it," Odette says. "*That is nothing*, she'll say, *compared to the Revolution.*"

"It undid my father," Niçois says. "He scrubbed his shoes long after the blood was gone. He cried all the time. I once slipped on a puddle he made with his tears. He was devastated by how viciously people hounded the nobility from their castles and mansions, dragged them naked through the streets and then cheered as their heads fell and rolled."

"Yes," Odette says. "My mother says the sound of a head falling to the ground echoes forever."

"And then, with no more rich people in Paris, there were no more orders for *faïence*. The *faïence* factories shut down. People left their homes— left Nevers!—and moved to Lyon to work at looms in dark textile factories, far from their parents and even from their children. My father felt it was his fault. Mother tried to soothe him. *Change is never free*, she would murmur.

"One morning two years ago, he kissed me on the forehead and said he was going for an early morning walk. *In your marriage shirt?* Mother asked him.

"He did more than take a stroll. He walked every street of Nevers. People remember seeing him. He patted every tree he passed and kissed every child he saw. Then he wandered down to the river.

He took an enormous *faïence* vase out of his boat and stepped from the muddy shore into the water, holding the vase tightly to his chest. We heard later that two fishermen yelled, *Stop! For the love of God!* But he didn't stop. He kept walking."

Niçois begins to cry. Odette touches his arm, as if to steady him.

After a minute he wipes his eyes on the back of his shirtsleeve. "The river poured over the lip of the vase. The water quickly filled the vessel, weighing my father down and pulling him deeper into the river, past its eddies and its currents, through shoals of fish, deeper and deeper, to its murky bottom."

"I'm so sorry," Odette says. It's what people say to her whenever one of Anneline's husbands dies.

"When my mother heard, she ran wailing through the streets," Niçois continues, as if in a trance. "Her screams were so loud and high pitched, they caused a horse to bolt. The horse went into the cathedral and knocked over a pew, which knocked over another, which knocked over another. Then, even though my mother can't swim, she dove into the river after my father. The fishermen who had tried to stop my father threw a net and dragged her out, choking, weeds tangled in her hair.

"I have not been able to eat fish from the Loire since. Sometimes, if a fishmonger has wares from the ocean, my mother gets me mackerel. You see, the fish of this river ate my father's flesh. Sometimes when I close my eyes, all I see are the pale clouds of their feasting."

Niçois and Odette sit in silence for a long while, staring out at the town.

"Thank you," Niçois says finally.

"You're thanking me? What for?"

"I have never told anyone all that. It feels good to put the pictures out there, out of my head. Spread them on the grass, like newly washed clothes."

Ten

Odette ties her new dishes into her apron. She and Niçois cross the bridge again and, after a short walk, arrive at the mill. They crouch on the stream bank and watch as the waterwheel whips the stream into froth. Odette plugs her ears against the noise of the millstones grinding the wheat. She can't understand how the mill doesn't fly apart with all the shuddering.

Drenched from the spray, the two climb higher up the stream bank and watch the flour thunder down the mill's chute, the white powder dusting the air so thickly that they cover their mouths, and sticking to their damp skin until they look like a pair of ghosts. They wipe each other clean with new oak leaves.

Away from the mill the world feels calm again. Niçois shows Odette the farm that sells the best milk, and the cobbler's, in case she ever has enough *sous* for leather shoes. He points out the tavern where Robespierre and Chaumette spoke to large audiences, and where now, even in the middle of the afternoon, a table of men sing "*La Marseillaise.*"

Niçois and Odette stand in the street, listening to the great song of the Revolution.

> *The day of glory has arrived!*
> *Against us, tyranny's*
> *Bloody banner is raised.*
> *To arms, citizens,*
> *Form your battalions.*
> *Let's march, let's march!*

They walk under the same stone arch that is painted on the plate. It is the Door of Paris, Niçois tells her, dedicated to France's win in the great battle of Fontenoy against the Austrian Succession. Then they are in Canot Place, a square where children scamper and men throng noisily around something that Odette can't see.

"The public notices," Niçois explains. "They're getting the latest news, from a duke's death to goats for sale. I don't know why they're so excited today."

Odette thinks she might know. She cranes her neck and, indeed, spies at the center of the crowd a head of haphazardly pinned chestnut hair.

"Give her room!" someone yells. It is Guillaume, the painter, perched on a ladder, touching up a sign. "Yes, she is beautiful, a lovely stranger, but let her breathe!"

Guillaume shakes his brush, spattering the hats and shoulders below with green. While the affected men shake their fists at him, something ripples through the crowd. Odette watches as her mother crawls out from the forest of legs. Anneline's cloak is snagged under someone's heel. She gives it a tug, lifts her skirt high and runs for freedom from the amorous mob.

A moment later a man bursts out of the crowd, looking wildly about. His hair is yellow and straight. His mustache and beard are unusually trim and tight on his face. His eyes are small, and his face twitches. He is like a dog catching a scent. Odette realizes with a start that it is the spy from the riverbank.

Anneline vanishes around a corner before the yellow-haired man spots her. The man looks left, right, high and low, then dives back into the crowd. He emerges moments later and, with the other men hollering after him, runs out of the square, clutching a piece of paper in his hand.

"I wonder what that was all about," Niçois says. He turns to Odette. "You look pale."

"I'm fine," she lies. She is shaken, in fact. She fights the overwhelming urge to run after her mother. It feels as though today she has entered a new world, and chasing her mother would only lead her back to the old one.

Perhaps her mother is right. Perhaps her notice will get a response in this town. But if it's from the yellow-haired man...He doesn't look friendly at all.

Odette is distracted from her worries when Niçois leads her through a small door cut into the large cathedral door. A door through a door! Hinges within hinges! She steps back out and in again, marveling.

Inside, the cathedral is cool and dark and musty—a little like the smell of a fresh grave, Odette thinks. Figures in rags doze in the pews. One grips an unlit candle in his dirty hands. Another holds a hat to his heart. Monks scrub the low stone steps leading up to the altar. The hems of their cloaks are dark from dragging in the water.

Pigeons sigh in the ceiling beams. One flaps across the wide transept, making a sound like cards being shuffled.

"I come here often in the summer," Niçois whispers as he and Odette sink into a pew. "To cool down. And sometimes Mother makes me attend Mass with her. Luckily, there's always a baby arriving in Nevers, so she can rarely go. In any case, she says our hearts are churches, and we can worship wherever we are."

"My mother doesn't like Mass," Odette says. She glances nervously at Niçois. "She doesn't, in fact, like the church."

Niçois clamps his hands onto his head and ducks, as if Odette's sacrilege might cause the ceiling to fall. Odette giggles. She makes the sign of the cross, as if this could save her from the tumbling stones. Niçois's eyebrows fly up, and he claps a hand over his mouth. The smack echoes in the church like cannon shot, which only makes the two laugh harder. Odette loves the feeling of her bones loose in her joints.

The monks stand to look for the disruptive heathens. Dark, wet circles on their cloaks mark the location of their knees. Niçois and Odette duck low and hide, barely breathing, until they hear the monks' brushes scrubbing the stairs again.

Niçois shows Odette the chapels that line the walls of the cathedral. Each one has a small altar. One displays a rib bone propped on red velvet, protected in a glass jar. A small sign claims that the bone belonged to a saint, Martin of Tours, who once used his sword to cut his cloak in two to keep a beggar warm. Odette suspects the bone is actually a goat's.

Another chapel holds the graves of a Nevers duke and a duchess. What was it like to be a duchess, Odette wonders, with a bed stuffed with goose feathers, and servants to make breakfast and lay the fire and pump the bathwater and haggle for the cheapest cut at the butcher? Wait! There would be no more cheap cuts. No more haggling. To have coins always at the bottom of your pouch, as if it were spring fed. The idea dizzies her.

Though Odette knows it would be wrong to *wish* to be a countess, richer than others (the revolutionaries put an end to that kind of inequality), surely to imagine the impossible wasn't a crime!

Something rustles in the chapel. Odette puts a finger to her lips and kneels low, expecting to find a mouse. Niçois listens. "Water," he says. "An underground stream. We had a very wet winter—so wet the butcher sold pigs' bladders for people to put their pocket watches in, to protect them from rusting. Unfortunately, one man was attacked by a hungry marten who sniffed out the bladder, which had not been perfectly cleaned."

"No!"

A monk shuffles out a small door at the back of the cathedral, letting in a blast of sunlight. Odette and Niçois, having had enough of the damp, dark air, hurry after him.

They leap across the threshold into the bright spring day.

Eleven

A few streets from the cathedral, in a triangular patch of grass under a leafy chestnut tree, stands an extraordinarily handsome donkey.

"He looks"—Odette takes a breath—"sad. And tired."

The donkey flinches. Flies buzz at its eyes. Niçois brushes them away. Only one remains, stuck fast in the thick syrup of a lonely tear. Niçois takes the fly between his finger and thumb, extracts it and places it in the grass. He rubs the donkey's legs. "There now, you're all right." He looks up at Odette. "I think his legs get sore. All the standing."

"Why doesn't he lie down?"

"I think he doesn't like to get dirty. He moaned a lot during all the rain last winter, when things got very muddy."

The donkey lays its big head on Niçois's bony shoulder and sighs elegantly.

"The strange thing is that he only brays at night," Niçois says. "And no one seems to own him. He just arrived in Nevers one day."

"I think he doesn't want to be a donkey," Odette says, remembering the Latin words.

Niçois laughs. "That's a funny idea."

Odette feels herself blush.

"There's nothing wrong with funny ideas," Niçois adds quickly.

"Have you ever imagined not being a person?" Odette asks, emboldened.

Niçois frowns. "That's a hard question. It hurts my brain—in a good way."

Odette knows what he means. When Félix asked her difficult questions—which was often—she felt like her head would pop off. Sometimes, when the question was too tough, she'd cry. Then Félix would break it into smaller questions. She tries this now with Niçois. "Can you imagine being something other than what you are?"

Niçois glances up. "I can somewhat imagine being this chestnut tree," he says, "lapping us with shadows. Or even one of those clouds, embroidering the sky. And maybe that fountain"—he points —"gurgling beneficently." He looks at Odette. "But no matter who or what I was, I feel that I would always be me."

Odette contemplates the donkey. She has a theory about what its problem is. The beast's desire to not be a donkey could be the result of a blow to the head.

Some years earlier, when they lived in Macon, Odette's mother had heard from a neighbor that Rose Bertin—Marie Antoinette's dressmaker— was passing through town. Anneline hurried out of the house, fevered to catch a glimpse of the renowned seamstress. At that same moment her fifth husband was returning to their cottage, after a long day of counting numbers at the bank. Not seeing him, Anneline threw open the gate and knocked him into the street. A cart promptly rolled over him, the horse stepping directly on his head.

After that he was very changed. He no longer recognized Anneline or Odette. He thought the night sky was a heavily salted bowl of mushroom soup and would try to reach it with a spoon. He had strange, obsessive desires that would make him weep. He wanted to iron an angel's gown, for example, or twirl the cottage they lived in on his finger like a spinning top. One evening he sobbed inconsolably because he could not see his bones— what he called his "inside basket."

He finally died from eating a roof slate. No one knew why he had done it, but once in a while Anneline still turns to Odette out of the blue and suggests a possible reason. "Perhaps he thought it was a Eucharist, and he wanted to take communion." Or: "Perhaps he thought he was a pigeon and needed stones for his gizzard, to grind up his food."

The donkey rubs his nose against Odette's shoulder. He seems to be drawn to her.

"You can stroke him," Niçois offers.

Odette is not inclined. She's too nervous. Instead, she looks into the donkey's eyes. "You made a lot of noise last night," she scolds. "Please be quieter tonight. Remember that people are sleeping, and we need to work hard tomorrow." She sizes up the donkey. "Why don't *you* work?"

Niçois gulps. "My father and a neighbor tried," he says quietly. "It was hopeless. If you put so much as a thatch of hay on this donkey's back, he collapses to the ground, wailing. All donkeys resist the pull of the rope, but this one doesn't just resist—he dances in protest. In fact, the dance teacher was called to watch, and then things got strange. The teacher cried out, *He knows the* passepied *and the* sarabande*!"*

Odette rolls her eyes. *What is with this town? Of course the donkey doesn't know the* passepied— *let alone the* sarabande. *Those are complicated dances. But if this donkey actually was calling out in Latin…*

Odette thinks of the goats and cows and horses she has known. Those animals all calmed when you spoke in smooth tones, and they cowered or bolted if you spoke suddenly or roughly. This animal, though, looks right at Niçois and Odette when they speak, its eyes moving from face to face. Its eyes are quicker than any horse's. It's as if there's a mind— a *nous*—at work.

As Niçois gathers grass from a nearby ditch to feed to Anne, Odette leans toward the donkey and whispers in his furry ear, "*Salve.*" Anne shows no sign of understanding. His ear doesn't twitch. He doesn't turn to look at Odette. *Ungulam pulsa*, Odette says. "Hello. Stamp your hoof." Anne does not move. He remains calmly regal in the dappled shadow of the chestnut tree. Odette feels entirely foolish.

"Well, he's a fine-looking beast," she finally says to Niçois. "Complainy. But a very fine beast underneath."

She really did say that.

Twelve

"May God sour your wine!"

"Oh, did I step on you? You are so small, I didn't see you."

"May your bread harden."

On their way home Niçois and Odette witness a fight at the city's largest fountain, between two water bearers—men who earn their *sous* delivering water door to door in casks. One had cut in line in front of the other and stepped on the other's toe while doing so.

"Why, you're smaller than Marie Antoinette's dog. Same squashed-in face too."

"May rats devour your brie."

"That dog got the bayonet, I believe. Immediately after its owner's head rolled."

"May your strongest hen lay stones."

A man in a large overcoat steps between them. Odette is startled to see it's the hand smeller. "His name is M. Mains," Niçois whispers to her.

"Brothers, you are fighting over, what, a few seconds, lost by one, gained by the other?"

"He stepped on my foot!"

"Then thank him. Pain reminds you you're alive."

"How could I see him? He's the size of a lap dog."

"Sir," M. Mains says. "Shout into your barrel."

The man who cut in line gamely puts his face to the opening of his water cask. "Coco!" he shouts. The crowd roars with laughter—Coco was the name of Marie Antoinette's dog.

"It is still empty, as you can hear," M. Mains says. "Cutting in line did not help you. Listen. Life is but a streak of light. If you hurry, you only meet darkness more quickly. Did Chaumette fall for nothing? Robespierre? All men are brothers. Embrace, unless you be not men."

The water bearers hang their heads, then clap their arms around each other's shoulders, apologize for their insults and withdraw their curses. When all is settled, M. Mains asks to smell their water-wrinkled hands.

"He was once a great professor in Paris," Niçois explains to Odette.

"So he told me. At the Sorbonne," Odette says.

"Yes. He studied hand smells and regional identity, whatever that is, but the university dismissed him."

"Why?"

"One afternoon, without permission, M. Mains leaped onto a stage and smelled the hands of a visiting guest. Not just any guest. The Pope."

"Oh no!"

"*The Holy Father's hands smell of prayer!* M. Mains yelled to the audience. Which would have been all right. But then he continued, *And Gorgonzola cheese.*"

Odette bursts out laughing.

"The audience laughed too," Niçois says. "But the Pope did not, and neither did the Sorbonne deans. M. Mains was fined for 'vulgar familiarity.' The Vatican believed his mention of Gorgonzola cheese, which is streaked with blue, was a blasphemous joke—"

"About the Pope's face! They say it's shattered with blue veins."

"The church claims the veins are from age, but everyone knows they come from the Pope's fondness for hazelnut liqueur. So M. Mains was hounded out of Paris. He came here to Nevers. He still attends Mass, though I don't think the Pope would be happy to hear that. He presses his nose to the church pew in front of him to smell the hands of all who have prayed there."

The water bearers wave their hands under M. Main's nostrils. He inhales deeply and smiles. The crowd leans in for his pronouncement. "Hickory. From the barrels you roll sloshing through the streets. I told you: you are brothers. Now get back in line."

The men do as they're told, each this time begging the other to go first.

Thirteen

When Odette gets back to their small home, she finds Anneline pale and shivering in bed. "I don't even have the strength to read *Aline et Valcourt*," her mother moans.

"You shouldn't have gone out. I told you," Odette says.

Anneline chokes out a wet cough.

"The man in the ridiculous blouse at the castle fundraiser had that cough!" Odette remembers suddenly. "The one who made the long speech. You didn't kiss him, did you?"

"Of course not. You know the law. Commit adultery, and it's the convent for life. Can you see me in a convent again?"

Odette can't. Her mother hates nuns—with good reason. And she knows nothing about gardening or folding laundry or dipping candles or sitting in silence, which is what nuns mostly do. And, of course, Anneline loves men. Helplessly. There are no men in convents.

Odette tucks her mother's cloak around her. Anneline murmurs something.

"Pardon?"

"I said, Thank you."

Odette doesn't know how to respond. Her mother has never thanked her before for anything.

Anneline rubs her head. "It hurts so much. There's a terrible bump."

Odette thinks of the husband who ate the roof slate after being crushed by the cart. Could Anneline's fall at the marketplace have something to do with her alarming gratitude?

"At least I have a foot warmer," Anneline says. She nods toward her feet, where the piglet and chick lie enfolded.

Tick-tick, Odette hears. The chicks must be hatching in the armoire.

Anneline widens her eyes. "Is that your stomach, daughter? Sometimes it makes such strange sounds."

No. For once Odette isn't hungry, even after running around all day with Niçois. She feels too warm and light. "That's the chicks coming out of their shells."

"Not already. I don't know what to do with babies."

"You do," Odette lies. She adds a handful of corn to the small pile in the armoire and tops up the water.

Anneline calls after her. "No, Odette. I don't know what to do with babies. You forget. I did not grow up in a normal family. I never had a mother."

Odette sits on the edge of the bed. Anneline smooths a strand of hair behind Odette's ear. Odette stiffens. Yes, she thinks, it must have been the fall that has brought on this tenderness. "I keep hearing the rock wall crashing down," Anneline says. "Even while I read *Aline et Valcour*, it rumbles through my mind. I even smell the dust and hear the cries of the people."

Odette feels her mother's forehead. "Your fever is not as bad as yesterday," she says. "How did things go with the notice?"

"People got excited—but about me more than the notice. I haven't completely lost my looks, I suppose."

"Of course not."

"I will have some of that broth now."

Odette serves the broth in the *faïence* cups. Taking care that her mother doesn't see Félix's knife, she cuts up an apple from last year's crop that she found still clinging to a tree, withered but edible. She fans out the slices on the *faïence* plate. Anneline slurps and chews and swallows. She points at the bare plate. "Who's that? She looks familiar."

But before Odette can answer, Anneline sighs and falls back on the bed. Soon she is lightly snoring.

Odette tidies the dishes and raises a fire, then lies down beside her mother and watches the sky darkening through the window.

A cart rumbles up the street, and the chatter of happy women fills the evening air. The cart stops just outside. Odette overhears farewells and friendly teasing. Niçois's mother, she surmises, being dropped off at the end of Hell day.

The road beneath the little house quiets. The apartment grows dark.

Odette falls asleep to the sound of chick after chick announcing itself. *Peep-peep, peep-peep,* like tiny carriage wheels needing oil.

Fourteen

Once again, in the thick dark of the Nevers night, Odette's sleep is disrupted by hoarse cries. Odette hurries to the window. She pulls hard on her braid, digs her fingernails into her arms and slaps her cheeks. She wants to be sure she is awake.

She turns her ear toward the hoary brays, listening for the flow of meaning within them. *Debeo homines eloqui.* Yes. The donkey is speaking Latin. Again, he goes on and on. Odette translates to herself. "I must speak. A donkey's loneliness is unbearable, but times are changing. For the first time in this donkey life, I do not feel alone."

The night swallows Anne's honks, and silence returns. But then, as if unable to restrain himself, the donkey speaks again. *Illa puella*, he brays. "That girl."

Odette flushes. She stares for a long time into the dark, threading Anne's words through her mind. Could he mean *her*? She considers calling out to him. But what would she say? *Adsum*? I am here? She doesn't want to further disrupt the sleepers of Nevers. Besides, what would the townspeople think of a girl who talks to a donkey?

She decides she will visit Anne the next day, on her own. Then she lies down again, claiming a part of Anneline's cloak for warmth. But she doesn't sleep long. Just before dawn the quiet is shattered again.

"Do thieves live in my house as worms invade an apple?" M. Gustave's feathered hulk fills the doorway. He is puffing from the climb up the stairs.

"It's Lisane's house," Odette corrects wearily.

M. Gustave shuffles his feet. "Then do thieves live in Lisane's house, as weevils in a block of cheese?"

Lighter steps are heard on the stairs, and the thin woman from the market rushes in, wearing a dirty, patched dress. "What did I tell you?" she screeches at

M. Gustave. She scowls at Anneline, who has been rudely awakened. "That's my piglet in your bed."

The woman dives toward the piglet, who shuffles backward on its trotters into Anneline's lap. The chick hops between the piglet and the woman, cheeping madly. The woman bats the ball of fluff out of the way. It tumbles dangerously close to the fire.

"Hey!" Odette yells. She gathers the trembling chick in her hand.

"That piglet is my property!"

"Yes, it is," Anneline mumbles groggily.

"Don't you deny it—"

"Take him," Anneline says. "I don't need another mouth to feed."

Odette grits her teeth. Anneline does not understand basic farming principles. Everything they fed the piglet would in turn feed them.

The woman leans toward Anneline and snatches up the animal. "You keep your hands off my little pig!" she yells. She turns and runs down the stairs with the little pig kicking and squealing under her arm.

"*You* keep your piglet from coming here!" Anneline yells after the woman.

The chick cheeps sorrowfully in Odette's hand.

M. Gustave shuffles awkwardly. He strokes his chin and mutters about beards being made of hair, not feathers, and how much better chickens are than people.

Odette reaches into her apron and places coins into his large, chubby hand. "For rent. And a roasting chicken," she says.

M. Gustave brightens. "I knew you hadn't stolen that piglet." He gazes at the chick. "You are a darling one." He strokes the chick's fuzzy head with a wide fingertip. "I wonder where you came from."

"It hatched yesterday," Odette says. "Lisane has several new chicks. I would like to keep them."

M. Gustave shakes the coins in his hand. "I suppose it's up to Lisane. What does she think?"

Odette can't fathom how to answer the question. "I don't know," she says. "She would probably like them to be close to her."

"You are right," says M. Gustave. "They should remain here. You know, there's nothing I like better than watching a chick crack out of its shell. I pretend it's me breaking through. It would have to be a large egg to hold me though, wouldn't it?"

"Well, bigger than…" Again Odette doesn't know quite what to say. But it doesn't matter. M. Gustave is utterly distracted, gazing at Anneline, who must be feeling better. She is reading her novel, chewing on the ends of her hair, tears streaming down her cheeks.

Finally, great, sweating M. Gustave bends toward the chick calming in Odette's hand and whispers, "You will be large like me one day." He raises his arms and flaps them, then heads out the door and down the steps to the street.

The morning sun breaks through the clouds and lights up the room. Odette takes note of the spots that need scrubbing. The shutters next door bang open, and a woman's friendly voice calls, "Wake up, son."

Odette looks at the *faïence* dishes lining the mantel, and, for the first time since she and her mother and Félix shared a cottage at the edge of a graveyard, she feels as though the house she lives in breathes, like something alive.

Fifteen

Niçois's story about being whipped by his father had reminded Odette that nettle tea is good for treating fever. Félix swore by it. He would gather it from the edges of the graveyard whenever she or Anneline was sick and boil the leaves until they were as slimy as seaweed.

As she heads down to the street to see if she can find some of the plant, Niçois leans out of his window. "Odette! Good news. My mother wants your help. She has work for you already. Today!"

"But what do I do?"

"Don't worry—Mother will tell you. For now she asked me to give you this." Niçois throws a grayish ball out the window. Odette catches it in her apron. It is a ball of wax, rippled where Niçois held it. Odette presses her fingers into the channels that his fingers made.

"Take the wax to the priest and get it consecrated," Niçois says. "It will be needed later on for the birth."

To get to the cathedral, Odette decides to cut through the alley that is always thick with M. Gustave's chickens. But when she turns into the little street, her heart freezes: the man with the yellow hair, trim mustache and twitchy face is talking to M. Gustave. A chicken clucks at the yellow-haired man's feet, but he kicks it out of the way. He wears leather shoes with buckles. The shoes are clearly from Paris, though the buckles are tarnished from age and misuse. Odette slips behind a pile of broken chairs. She watches, heart pounding, as the yellow-haired man drops something into M. Gustave's hand. Odette hears the music of coins.

M. Gustave puts his other hand on his belly and bows deeply, drawing back his right leg so that the toe of his *sabot* scrapes across the cobblestones. "At your service," Odette hears him say. The yellow-haired man hurries away. Odette ducks farther behind the chairs until he has passed her—so closely that she notices the rags tucked into the backs of his too-large shoes to make them fit.

Outside the cathedral the priest is gazing up at the sculptures that crown the great door. Most have no heads. The noses are broken off others. Many are also missing fingers or entire hands. "You can still recognize Saint John without his head," the priest says with a sigh. "He carries a book. And Saint Peter holds a key. Those revolutionaries had no shame. They beheaded the saints the same as they beheaded the rich. Scoundrels. But I understand what they wanted. I have been to bishops' parties where wine flows and everyone prattles on about how well they know Cardinal so-and-so. While beggars sleep in gutters!"

Odette holds out the lump of wax.

"Ah," says the priest. "Another baby on its way?"

Odette nods.

The priest waves his hand over the ball. "God, Lord, king of ages," he intones. "All-powerful and All-mighty, you who made everything. We beseech you to make powerless, to banish and drive out, every diabolical power and machination, and keep all evil from the keyhole." He looks at Odette. "There. It will not let the devil pass."

On her way home Odette makes a detour to visit Anne. He is asleep, standing under the chestnut tree.

Excuscita! Odette says. "Wake up."

Anne's head lifts. Did he understand her? Odette can't tell. He might simply have been startled by her voice.

"I'm sorry you don't like being a donkey," Odette tells him in her best Latin. She speaks quietly and tries not to move her lips. She doesn't want any townspeople passing by to think she's daft. Anne shivers, as if his skin is loose on him. He nibbles the grass at his feet. Does he hear her?

"You mentioned a girl last night," Odette says in Latin. "Was it me?"

Anne continues to eat the grass.

Just then a group of noisy children run up. They throw handfuls of long grass at Anne and jeer. "Lazy donkey!"

"That isn't nice!" Odette scolds.

The children glare at her. "Who are you?" one asks.

"Just…nobody."

"Everyone is someone," the child says.

"Everyone is someone," a bigger boy repeats. "Everyone is someone, and someone is everyone!"

The boy pretends he's enormous. In a deep voice he shouts, "I am everyone!" He looms over the smallest child.

The children run away laughing.

"I have to go," Odette tells Anne.

Anne still doesn't respond. But as soon as Odette steps away, he clamps his teeth onto the hem of her dress.

Promitto revenire, Odette says, wresting her dress from between his teeth. "I promise I'll come back."

Using an elm leaf to protect her hand, Odette stops to pick enough nettles for tea. Next she begs a bone at the butcher's back door, still distracted by thoughts of the strange donkey. All the way home, she puzzles over their encounter. Anne did not seem to understand her, yet he wanted her to stay.

She feels sure now that Anne did bray in Latin during the night. After all, she does not have a fanciful imagination, and she had slapped her cheeks to make sure she wasn't dreaming. Niçois said that Anne only brays at night. So perhaps the donkey doesn't understand things during the day?

It is all so impossible though. It is ridiculous! Still, she has to trust her own senses.

Odette is jolted from her musing by Niçois shouting from his window as she approaches the little house.

"The birth will be this evening. I'll come and get you when it's time. Hang on to the wax until then."

Odette prepares tea and broth for Anneline, and as her mother takes feeble sips of each, heavy footsteps once again pound up the stairs.

M. Gustave enters and bows. "A widow requests your presence."

Odette studies him carefully, suspiciously. Can they trust him after the conversation she witnessed between him and the man with the yellow hair?

"Mme Geneviève is her name," M. Gustave continues. "She is old, so she cannot come here. She lives past the Port de Médine, in the woods, and wants to talk to you about Cluny. About a bridge?"

Anneline leaps out of the bed. She grips M. Gustave's enormous face between her hands until he looks like a codfish. "Is this really true?"

"Do you call me a liar, Madame?" M. Gustave bubbles.

"No! You have simply delivered such good news it is hard to believe." She turns to Odette. "We must go. Immediately."

"You aren't well enough," Odette says. "I'll go, and I will tell you what the old woman says."

"The nettle tea has restored me. And the broth. I am going. M. Gustave, you have delivered a fine message. But I regret I have no coin to give you."

"I think he has enough coins," Odette murmurs.

M. Gustave shuffles on his feet. Then he breathes in deeply, his nose whistling and his eyebrows quivering. "The broth smells delicious," he says.

So Odette and Anneline wait while M. Gustave, dipping his head into the pot like a bird, slurps up every last drop of bone broth and then washes it down with nettle tea.

Sixteen

Anneline talks feverishly for the entire walk to Mme Geneviève's, remembering the summer afternoon she and Odette boated to find the box. She counts the times she has put up a poster in a new town—eleven—and never heard back. And she wonders, as she often has, what had been in the mysterious box. She lists off the husbands who had wealthy families. Claude. Marcel. Edouard. And the one with the bristles of dark hair in his ears—what was his name again?

Geneviève's blue cottage is nestled in a grove of small pine trees. Anneline raises her knuckles to the door, but she doesn't knock. "I can't," she says. She gnaws her fingernails.

Odette steps forward and raps on the rough wood. A voice on the other side calls out weakly, "Enter."

The cottage is dimly lit. It has a dirt floor, and the air is thick with smoke and the stench of dung. Through a window cut in the far wall, two oxen bob their horned heads into the main room. Between husbands, Odette and her mother have lived with oxen this way, their stalls pressed close to the house. Their massive bodies warm the cottage, and the beasts provide company too.

Sausages hang over the fireplace, drying. The mantel is lined with candlesticks, shuttles and spools for weaving, a *faïence* jug with its spout knocked off—like the noses of the saints at the cathedral, Odette thinks—pewter cups and a bronze sculpture of a porcupine with holes where its quills should be. It is a match holder, the kind Odette has seen in rich people's homes. She is surprised to see one here. The rich can afford matches, but everyone else makes do with borrowed embers.

The table is edged with bowl-shaped scoops dug into the wood, into which soup can be poured and meals served to save using dishes. The long table is heaped mostly with tools—tongs, hammers—but also books, bones, scraps of leather and tin. A clock's pellet heartbeat punctures the silence. The clock surprises Odette the way the match holder did. It is an article for the wealthy, who have the leisure to measure their days with time rather than chores.

A bed is pushed close to the fireplace, and deep in its blankets is a wrinkled face framed by gray hair. Small, dark eyes peer at Anneline and Odette over the lip of a blanket. "The clock and the porcupine were gifts," the woman explains. She must have noticed Odette looking at them. "Gratitude for service. I had strength once. I spent it all in the houses of the rich, polishing their silver, keeping their fires burning, tending their children. Ever since I hung up my apron and walked away, my body has begged for sleep. But I have so much to do. So many ideas to make real. Earthly answers to airy questions. Inventions.

"I've devised a candle holder that collects the melted wax into a form for a new candle. You turn it over when the candle melts away, and, *voilà*! You have a fresh one. I am working on a match that you can light in the rain, soap that makes your hair free of scalp snow, and a liquid that will hold the heat of the sun so you can use it later." The woman sits up. "I was just having a nap. Now, who are you?"

"You called for us," Odette says.

"I never called for anyone."

"The large man said you had," Anneline says.

"M. Gustave," Odette reminds her mother. Sometimes Anneline doesn't even remember *her* name. She has called Odette Colette, Huguette, Henriette and Juliette, and many times simply *ma fille*.

"Do you know anything about a key and a package left in Cluny some years ago?" Odette asks Mme Geneviève.

"And a box under the struts of a bridge," Anneline adds breathlessly. "It was empty when we found it." She falls weakly to her knees and presses her face against Mme Geneviève's blankets. "Please, please, please."

"Mother," Odette chides, embarrassed. For all her faults and all her troubles, Anneline has never shown such weakness, such desperation. Such exhaustion. Is this another result of the bump on her head?

Mme Geneviève looks at Anneline with distaste, then says decisively, "I don't know what you're talking about."

But as she speaks, the old woman glances at Odette and nods conspiratorially. A thrill runs through Odette. It appears that Mme Geneviève knows exactly what they are talking about.

The clumsy conversation is interrupted by the ring of horse bells. Then "Whoa!" cries a man's voice outside the door. "Yoo-hoo, *ma tante*! It's me!" Odette hears the rider drop to the ground. When he appears at the door, her heart drops. It's the man with the yellow hair. Sharp nose, trim beard, tarnished shoe buckles.

"Now I see," the old woman says under her breath. She presses a smile onto her face. "Nephew Renard! It has been a long time. I wonder what brings you here today—at this exact moment that I have my first visitors in two moons?"

"A delightful coincidence, *ma tante*." The man's voice is smooth, as if it has been dipped in oil.

When his eyes land on Anneline, still on her knees beside Geneviève's bed, he reaches for her hand and pulls her up. He kisses her hand, then tracks his lips up her wrist. "Who are you, ravishing creature?"

It is true that Anneline looks particularly beautiful today. The fever has added color to her cheeks, and the sweat has made her skin glow and her hair curly. But Odette suspects that the man is more interested in the notice Anneline posted than in her beauty. Anneline giggles coquettishly. "Well, who are you, sir?"

"Nothing without you. Tell me your name and then every detail about you—how you feel, what is important to you, your favorite kind of day."

"This may be my favorite kind of day," Anneline says, smiling at Renard.

Renard looks into Anneline's eyes. "It is my favorite day yet."

Odette despairs, watching her mother gaze at Renard—a spy, a smarmy briber, a manipulator. Anneline had seemed to be making such progress since arriving in Nevers, but Odette knows that once Cupid has landed his arrow, there is nothing she can say or do to divert her mother.

As Renard and Anneline babble giddily, the old woman rises laboriously from her bed and hobbles over to the oxen. She signals for Odette to approach. "Are you Anneline's maid?" she whispers.

"I am her daughter."

"Are there other children?"

"No."

Mme Geneviève looks over at Anneline, then at Odette. "Are you sprung from her loins?"

"Yes."

"You are sure?"

It is common for children whose mothers died in childbirth to be raised by relatives or neighbors, Odette knows. Still, she wonders why Mme Geneviève feels the need to press the issue. "Yes, I am certain."

The woman touches Odette's cheek. "You are a serious one. And, I think, clever."

Renard has noticed them now, and he seems alarmed. "What are you talking about?" he cries.

He drops Anneline's hand as if it were a hot coal, hurries across the room and barges between Odette and his aunt, pulling himself up onto the sill of the oxen's window.

Anneline stares after him, insulted. Then she rouses herself.

"Madame," she says. "Do you now remember sending for us? I know that age addles the mind. And it clearly puckers the face—have you ever heard of Egyptian oil?"

Mme Geneviève bristles. "*Je suis désolée*, but it appears you have come all this way for nothing."

Renard leaps down from the sill. "Do you not have something you could tell them?"

"I could tell them about my latest invention—"

"No, *ma tante*. The package. The box under the bridge. With the book in it."

Odette starts. "Book?"

"Book?" Anneline repeats.

Mme Geneviève crosses the room and crawls slowly back under her blanket. "This is all very confusing," she says weakly. Quick as a moth's wing, she winks at Odette, then closes her eyes and begins to snore.

"*Tante!*" Renard barks. "We are—this woman is looking for something. If you can help her find it…"

Mme Geneviève doesn't stir. Renard takes hold of her shoulder and shakes, but the old woman remains deeply, impossibly asleep.

As Anneline and Renard grouse about muddle-headed old people and how disgustingly they snore, Odette gives the oxen a handful of forage. Mme Geneviève clicks her tongue between snores, and when Odette looks up she is startled to see that the old woman's eyes are half open. Odette is being studied. "*Au revoir*, madame," she whispers.

Mme Geneviève shuts her eyes again.

Outside, Renard helps Anneline onto his horse. "I will take you home, most attractive one." He climbs onto the saddle in front of her. Anneline puts her arms around his waist as he shakes the reins and clicks his tongue.

Odette walks home alone.

Seventeen

"Odette!" Niçois calls up from the street with urgency. "This instant! In Rue Casse-Cou. The lady is having her eighth baby. Mother says she's frightened."

Odette hurries to the window. "Frightened?"

"The lady's mother died when she delivered *her* eighth child, which was the lady herself. I'll show you the way. Don't forget the wax!"

Odette pats her apron. "I have it."

As Niçois leads her through the narrow streets of Nevers, he tells her quickly what he knows about childbirth. "Keep the room dark and warm. A wet cloth on the mother's forehead is nice. She may want to bite it. Stay calm."

They arrive at an alley filled with fretful wailing.

"That's her," Niçois says. Odette gulps. Niçois squeezes her hand and leads her to a stairwell. At the top is a battered door. "Knock three times. No more. Or Mother will think it's the devil. And make sure to tell the woman that all will be well."

"But I don't know that it will be."

"It will be," Niçois says.

Odette climbs the stairs as quickly as she can, her body stiff with fear. She knocks three times at the door. The woman who answers is wholly unlike Anneline. She is solid and ruddy, as if she works in the fields. Her eyes are lively. She stands with her feet apart and her hands on her hips and sizes up Odette. Her smile shows off large, crooked teeth.

"You look steady and sincere," she tells Odette. "I think you will be a good help. Now you need to know, when a baby is being born nothing can stop it. Every moment matters. You will see. Time slows down, but every second is filled to the brim. Your first job is to fill each keyhole in the apartment with wax to stop the devil getting through. Next untie all the knots in this home so the baby can sail easily into the world. Can you manage that?"

Odette nods.

"Then you will be by my side with clean rags and fresh water and anything else I ask you for. You may have to shoo the others away—the children and the husband."

"Yes, madame."

"Please call me Marie-Claire. And try to smile a little."

Odette obediently shapes her lips so that the corners turn upward.

"Not bad."

Marie-Claire leads Odette into a small room where children of all sizes, some wearing pants but no shirt, others wearing shirts but no pants, jostle around a bed that smells of rotten hay. The woman in the bed moans to the man kneeling beside her, "I won't make it this time, Henri."

"You'll have to!" the man says cheerfully. "Who will make the soup if you don't?"

"Henri. I mean it," the woman says. "God is calling me."

"Then I don't believe in God," Henri says.

The children suck in their breaths. "Henri!" the woman admonishes. But the fear washes from her face.

"Now, now," Marie-Claire says. She glances at Odette and quietly points to the frayed ribbons in the woman's hair. "God is all around us, and God is helping you."

Odette unknots the woman's hair and lays out the hair ribbons in neat pink lines along the windowsill. The curtain is held back with a length of hemp rope—Odette undoes this too. Some of the children's shirts are tied shut at the neck, so Odette undoes these strings while the children stand patiently. They have been through this before.

In the kitchen a rope of garlic bulbs hangs from the ceiling, their stems braided together. *Are braids knots?* To be certain, Odette removes the garlic from its hook and unwinds the stems, laying each bulb separately on the kitchen table, the long stems parallel to each other. She then undoes her own braid and winds her hair into a chignon.

Then she is called by Marie-Claire to stroke the woman's head and hum to her. When at last

Marie-Claire says the baby's arrival is imminent, the oldest child hands Odette a length of white linen, saying it was washed that morning and has flapped on the clothesline all day in the sunshine, and that every one of her mother's babies has been caught in this same cloth. "Including me."

It is the finest linen Odette has ever touched. It is like holding air. She has been in houses with good cotton and expensive linens, with long curtains and lacy tablecloths, houses free of clamor, so it is strange to touch the finest cloth here in this chaotic place. She looks at the mother, who is tearful, terrified, and at the woman's husband, who murmurs in a bossy way that the woman seems to need. "You will let this baby into the world. And you will remain here with her. And with us."

The children are finally still. They promise to be quiet and are allowed to stand around the bed. Each grips someone else's hand. Odette is unsure whether they hold hands to give or receive comfort. With a jolt she realizes that it is both at once—like a river flowing in two directions. As if they all share a heart.

There is warmth and calm in the room, a gentle pulse that Odette recognizes. From where though?

She thinks of Félix. She nearly smells dirt. Yes. It is what passed between her and Félix when it was just the two of them talking in the graveyard, or singing together as they walked home, she on his shoulders. Funny that now, in a room where life is about to find light for the first time, she would remember Félix, who was so often waist deep in the dark earth, preparing an "upside-down bed," as he called a grave.

Life enters. Out of the dark and wet, from between the woman's legs, like a flower's shoot in spring, head first. To Odette, though, the silence is terrible. Marie-Claire takes the small bluish bulb in her hands and turns it, pulling gently, until, like a tassel unfurling, the rest of the baby—shoulders, chest, arms, legs—spirals out of its mother's body. The babe is wet and glistening, like a pit squeezed from a peach. No, Odette thinks, like a *peach* squeezed from a peach. A miracle.

The baby gasps for breath. Odette lets out her own with great relief. Marie-Claire holds the baby up for all to see, and there, high in the air, the baby finally wails. Everyone cheers. Marie-Claire lowers the baby to its mother's heart, and its pink mouth, small as two rose petals, latches quickly onto its mother's nipple.

The baby sucks and whistle-breathes through its tiny nostrils, then gulps and sighs sweetly.

The father, Henri, counts the baby's toes— "*un, deux, trois, quatre, cinq, six, sept, huit, neuf, dix*"—then bustles across the room, opens the bedroom window and shouts into the night, "New feet! New feet! To run the streets of Nevers!"

A couple of men wandering late in the streets shout up, "*Félicitations!*" As if in response, Anne's brays wind through the streets. The children of the family laugh.

"He's happy too," one says. But Odette knows the truth. Anne, as usual, is only complaining about his lot.

Blattae liberiores quam me sunt! "Moths have more freedom than me!"

"It is a girl," Marie-Claire announces, and then she mouths across the room to Odette, "Maybe."

They leave the family to rejoice together, and as they organize Marie-Claire's bags for the walk home, Marie-Claire explains that the baby is not a usual girl. "It happens every thousand births or so that a child has genitals for both a girl and a boy, or some of one and a few of the other. In some towns such a child is sent away and never seen again. But I fight for them," Marie-Claire says. "Guess why?"

Odette has never heard of such a thing. She doesn't know what to say.

Marie-Claire smiles. "I'm one myself. For some reason, I was lucky. My parents treasured me. They said it didn't matter to them—that they knew nothing of the ways of God and wouldn't presume to. My husband loved the way I am. He was not a bore. He knew that everyone was equal but different." Marie-Claire sighs. "Stoke the fire in the kitchen, please, and put some broth on. The mother will need her strength."

Odette adds coals to the fire and hangs a pot above it that she has filled with water, carrots, potatoes and onions. She returns to the bedroom, where Marie-Claire is explaining about the new baby. "We will say she is a girl today, but one day she may want to be a boy. That is her power."

The family, overjoyed that the mother has not died in childbirth, accepts the baby readily.

Odette watches as Marie-Claire feels the woman's forehead. She pinches the mother's arms and cheeks to make the color return. She gives the family instructions: broth and rest for the mother, and a daily dusting of the baby's belly button with powdered cumin.

On their way out the midwife spies the garlic bulbs laid out with precision on the kitchen table. Laughing a little, she grips Odette by the shoulders and says, "Maybe *that*'s why we had such a perfect birth. I believe you will be good for the babies of Nevers."

It is nearing dawn when Odette and Marie-Claire finally step out into the street. The dark sky richens with blue. Marie-Claire hands Odette a small basket. A chill ripples through her. It is not just any basket. It looks exactly the same as the one carried by the girl on the *faïence* plate.

"The afterbirth is inside," Marie-Claire tells her. "You saw it come out after the baby? The placenta. An entire organ that grows to feed a baby while it is in the womb. It is the baby's first mother, some like to say. Take it to one of the monks at the cathedral. He will bless it and burn it and then have the ashes scattered in the church graveyard. Have you seen how beautifully the trees grow there?"

Eighteen

Odette decides she will visit Anne again on her way back from the cathedral. But as she approaches, a very large chicken crests the hill from the opposite direction. It is M. Gustave in his feathered cape. It looks to Odette as though he has drunk a lot of wine. She ducks behind the nearby fountain as M. Gustave hurries toward Anne.

"Hello, donkey," he burbles. "Hello, hello, hello. Such a moon last night. A glowing egg. Now for the sun to arrive, the glorious yolk."

M. Gustave is speaking so loudly that Odette can hear every word. "Like a great petal, your ear," he says to Anne, "the petal of a great, gray flower."

Anne tries to step sideways, but M. Gustave puts a heavy arm around the donkey's neck and holds him fast.

Odette listens, horrified, as the large man pours out his secrets.

"I did not bathe once this year," M. Gustave confides. "I am lonelier than an unhatched chick. By mistake last night I relieved my bladder into my chamber pot. You know that's where I keep my coins. Now they will rust. Normally I stand at my window if I need to release in the night. The old people tease me about the dark streak along the slates and the strange moss that grows there."

Odette pulls her apron over her head to hide her face and prepares to dart. But M. Gustave's next words freeze her in place. "Recently a stranger with hair like straw paid me *sous* to relay a message to a girl and her mother."

Odette's ears burn.

"The girl and her mother are new to town. They live in the house that floats over Rue de la Porte de Croux. I said it was mine, and now they pay me rent. The mother is beautiful. I don't normally notice women, beautiful or otherwise. I love hens. It has been that way for a long time. Hens are sleek and busy and easy to pick up. They are warm under the arm. They are better than a bed warmer, I have discovered. Yes, they foul the bed, but it is dry by morning. It is a joy to lie there and stroke their soft feathers as their eyes eclipse with sleep. They purr, you know. Better than a cat…

"The man paid me to deliver dull news, that is all. That someone wanted to see the beautiful woman and her daughter. The coins he placed in my hand were sticky, which made me wonder how he earned them. He was not gentle. He looked like a gentleman, but he was not gentle. *Do not mention me*, the stranger growled. *Do not describe me to anyone…*"

Odette hears the baker pushing his car through the streets, calling out, "Baguette, brioche!"

M. Gustave is winding up, and he speaks quickly. "I have wanted to be a chicken since I was a boy. I practice. I make my eyes as small as I can. I eat corn. For a long time I swallowed a spoonful each day of the oyster shells I feed my hens to make their eggs strong. Lately I have been eating pebbles. I pray at the cathedral. I light a candle if I have a coin and say, *Dear God, if you have pity, bless me with a gizzard."*

M. Gustave strokes Anne's neck with a trembling hand, whispers, "Farewell, brother," then chases after the baker. Odette hears him call, "I hope you won't mind that my coins are a little damp."

She is exhausted after the long night and decides to visit Anne later. She had better head home. Anneline will be needing her. Anne, surprised by Odette's sudden emergence from behind the fountain, stares after her with surprising feeling, as though his large gray donkey heart were flushing red.

Nineteen

Anneline's fever is down, but although she is nearly over her flu, she still isn't eating much, because she is in love. Odette is discouraged to see the signs she has so often seen before. Anneline spends the morning brushing her hair and reading *Aline et Valcour*, sighing, "Renard, Renard, Renard." Anneline asks Odette to launder her clothes because Renard is taking her for an afternoon stroll.

As she scrubs her mother's dress and bloomers against the rocks at the edge of the river, Odette tries not to think about the waterlogged bones of the Roman soldiers below—or of those of Niçois's father. She wrings out the clothes and lays them on the grass. With the coins from helping

Marie-Claire with the previous night's birth, she has bought a large ball of wool. Now, sitting in the spring sunshine, facing the river, she starts to knit a blanket.

"I will bet that your hands smell like lanolin," a voice chimes behind her. Lanolin, Odette knows, is the wax that oozes from sheep. Wool is sticky with it. "And of hickory. Or perhaps those needles are carved from cherry wood?" M. Mains swoops toward Odette's hands, but she quickly drops her knitting and sits on them.

"Apologies," M. Mains murmurs. He joins her on the grass. "I really should ask permission. But I am excited. I have had an excellent few days of research.

"Early this morning the boy who guides carriages at night let me smell his hands. The hand that holds the lantern smelled of the oily smoke that rises from the wick. But the other hand smelled of night air, from the boy's beckoning the driver along—night air and a bitter smell, the coins that are the coach driver's payment. I also smelled the fishmonger's hands. One smelled of fish, the other of his knife's oaken handle. I plan to write a new treatise about the kinds of occupations for which one hand smells different from the other."

Odette is wary of M. Mains, but as someone whose own hands are often busy, she can't help being fascinated by his reports.

"Later I smelled the mayor's hands. I thought they would smell of ink and paper, but they smelled of claret! And I finally smelled the formidable Mme Source's hands. She is the woman who lives on the edge of town, her hair a perfectly engineered beehive? If a well is to be built, Mme Source finds the water. She divines. She is beautiful." M. Mains blushes. "I mean in an academic way. I have long wanted to smell her palms. They smell of beef, mushrooms, red wine and pearl onions. You know what that all adds up to, don't you? Our city's most famous recipe. Boeuf bourguignon. The same as my mother's hands. The smell of home."

Odette thought of the lanolin on her hands. What other smells would there be? Cumin. Garlic. Bone broth. Elm leaf. Fresh grass. The smells of work. Yes. As she suspected, she is made of work.

"On my way back to town," M. Mains continues, "I knocked on some cottage doors, and in one house

I met a very interesting woman. Her hands smelled of wax and oxen. And sunlight! She told me she has been trying to make a liquid that will capture sunlight. An amazing idea."

"Mme Geneviève!" Odette exclaims.

"That was her name, yes. She gave me a letter to deliver. No, not a letter. She called it a message. She wanted me to be sure to tell the recipient that it was a message, not a letter. It is for a young girl named Odette. Do you know her?"

"I *am* her!"

"This is a coincidence then," M. Mains says. "Well, not really, if I am forced to think about it like a scholar. I've talked to thirty girls your age already, and every one of them had a different name from yours. Not one of them let me smell their hands either."

"May I have the letter?"

"Yes, of course." M. Main produces a damp, wrinkled page from his vest pocket. "But it's a message. Not a letter. She really wanted me to explain that." He studies Odette, taking in her torn skirt and dirty apron. "I can read it to you, if you—can't."

"I can read," Odette answers between clenched teeth.

Félix taught her. He had first taken her small finger and run it along the grooves chiseled in the headstones. "*A*," he would say. "Shaped like an animal with a triangular head and two legs. *F*. A flower with two petals. *V*. Shaped like a valley." Then he would send her among the gravestones to find the letters she had learned. She would mark the stones with dandelions, then lead Félix to them. He would read all the words on the gravestone aloud, emphasizing the letters she had found.

One day he had asked her something new. "Look for *N* and *É* together. *NÉ*." Later he instructed Odette, "Find the letters *M*, *O*, *R* and *T* all in a row beside each other."

Her legs had grown longer by then, and she leaped over the gravestones as she looked for the letters. She found them. In fact, she discovered they were on nearly every gravestone. These were words, Félix had explained, families of letters. *NÉ* meant "born." *MORT* meant "dead."

She tries not to snatch the note from M. Mains's hand, which, she thinks to herself, will smell of rag paper. "Thank you," she says, hoping he will be on his way.

When M. Mains lingers, Odette collects her mother's clothes, even though they remain damp, and gets to her feet.

"Since you've been washing clothes as well as knitting, your hands will smell of the Loire and the algae that thickens it. It is the longest river in France. But length doesn't have a smell," M. Mains says to her.

"I suppose it doesn't," Odette says. She starts up the bank. "Thank you again for the letter."

"Message," M. Mains corrects. "And you could thank me by letting me smell your hands."

"No!"

At the top of the bank Odette looks back at M. Mains. Perhaps she should have let him smell her hands after all. But he has moved on. He charges toward a fisherman by the river's edge, calling out, "Your pole! Is it made of elm or oak?"

Odette wants to read the message in private. But Anneline is home waiting for her clothes, so she won't be alone there. Odette finds her way to the cathedral and sits in the chapel beside the duchess's tomb. She hears again the water trickling under the floor. It calms her.

She unfolds the message and reads:

> *a delIght to Meet yoU yeSTerday*
> *i am Sorry about thE confusion*
> *plEase accept mY apOlogies hUmble*
> *Nevers shOuld Welcome you*
> *I love how LETTERS make words, don't you?*
> *mme geneviève*

Quite a strange note, Odette thinks. It was nice of the old woman to apologize for the peculiar visit, but why put M. Mains through all the trouble of finding her for such a simple message?

Odette stares at the stone sculpture of the duchess on top of her grave, at the long, smooth fingers that never washed clothes or pinched a candlewick to snuff out a flame but touched the hands of dukes while dancing the *allemande* in large rooms with lamplight and plates of food of all kinds...

A monk bursts into the chapel. Odette leaps up from the pew, startled, and her mother's clothes fall to the floor. The monk takes a handful of candles from a ledge and backs out of the chapel. "Washer girl," he says, noting the damp bundle of clothes, "I did not mean to frighten you. My humble apologies."

Odette stands and curtsies. "It is fine."

"Again, my humble apologies," the monk repeats.

That's funny, Odette thinks. Mme Geneviève had offered humble apologies too. No, she'd said it differently. She'd said *apologies humble*. Backward.

Odette reads the message again. Why had Mme Geneviève written that bit about letters and words, with *letters* all in capitals, and not used capitals where they were supposed to be? Félix had taught Odette that capital letters should only ever be at the start of words. Gravestones were exceptions— all the words on gravestones were in capitals, but that was because capital letters, with their straight lines, were easier to make with the chisel's flat blade.

After leaving the chapel, Odette has an idea. She'll stop at the blacksmith's on the way home and hold her mother's clothes near the fire to dry while she pretends to be interested in watching the blacksmith work.

The blacksmith's hammer falls steadily, like a great heartbeat, making sparks and ash fly. Every dozen swings, Odette turns her mother's dress and bloomers over in her hands. The blacksmith's dark beard is beaded with sweat, and the large man frequently wipes his runny nose on his sleeve. Every so often he stops hammering to fish a kerchief from a pocket and mop his brow.

"A kerchief around your forehead would stop the sweat from rolling into your eyes," Odette blurts. Félix wore a kerchief when he dug in the summer heat, she remembers. "It's better than a hat, because the heat can still escape through the top of your head." Odette takes a dark rag from a hook nearby. "This would work."

The blacksmith bends low and lets her tie the rag around his head. "Not too tight!" he squeaks. The joke makes her laugh. When she is done, the blacksmith strings a rope between two hooks. "Hang the clothes here to dry, and go and play, as young girls should, while my fire does its magic."

Thanking him shyly, Odette flings her mother's clothes over the rope and runs, not to play with the children in the square—she is too old for that

—but to the mill. She was too proud to scavenge oats when Niçois was with her, but now she fills her apron greedily.

On her way back to the forge, she gathers wild chamomile flowers to dry for tea and fresh bilberries. She shares these with the blacksmith, who is happy with how the kerchief is working.

"Ever since I turned forty, my eyebrows have not been as thick as they were," he tells Odette. "The moisture runs right through them—like when the Loire breaks its banks."

Odette laughs.

"Right into my eyes," the blacksmith continues. "It stings like onion juice. That's what sweat is, isn't it? Our sourness, boiled out of us? But this rag"—the blacksmith lifts the cloth from his head and wrings it, making the fire spit—"stops the flow. You are an angel."

The blacksmith reaches for her mother's clothes. Odette leaps between the clothes and his soot-black fingers. "Allow me!"

"They are lovely clothes. They belong to a lady, I can tell. One who may have fallen on hard times, but still."

"My mother," Odette tells him, folding the clothes neatly.

"Did fate or luck bring you to our capital city?"

Odette's ears fill with the rumble of the tall stone wall. "The past."

The blacksmith smiles. "The past delivered all of us to where we are, didn't it?" He raises his hammer, readying to strike. "Though you could say the future brought us here too."

"Is that a letter?" Odette points to the piece of metal the blacksmith shapes on his anvil.

"Yes, for the butcher's sign. I made it wrong the first time. I made it little. But the mighty butcher wants a big one. A capital *B*."

"A capital *B* is a *bisou*—a kiss," Odette says, repeating what Félix once said while teaching her to read. "Like two lips seen from the side."

"Yes!" the blacksmith says, puckering his lips and kissing the hot air.

Odette stands transfixed as he turns the capital *B* in the fire, hammers it into shape and quenches it in a bucket of water, making it fizz.

Twenty

As she winds through the narrow streets toward home, Odette thinks about Geneviève's note. It is so strangely written. Why were the capital letters scattered, then rammed together suddenly in *LETTERS*?

As she approaches the apartment, she hears someone screech, "Witch! Naked witch!"

Odette hurries up the stairs to find her mother in bed with her knees drawn up and *Aline et Valcourt* laid over her chest for modesty. The skinny woman leans over her, wagging a bony finger. "You bewitched my piglet," the woman shrieks. She pulls the pink creature from a bag hanging over her shoulder. "Look at him. He hasn't eaten or moved since you kidnapped him. I've tried everything. Tickled, yelled, pushed corn into his mouth, dunked him in cold water…"

"Cold water! Poor thing," Anneline says. Like little pink sails, the piglet's ears turn toward her voice. "One of our chicks has the same illness. Listlessness. Won't eat or sleep. Stares into space, shivering."

Six chicks in all have hatched from Lisane's eggs. Five are healthy and strong, pattering about and drinking and eating. But the first chick, the one that arrived prematurely, is not well. It drowses on the bed, barely able to keep its eyes open. Odette warns her mother constantly not to roll over onto it.

"Where is the chick?" Odette asks now, searching the bed with some panic.

"I put it in the cupboard with the others," Anneline says. "I couldn't bear its sad eyes any longer."

Odette throws Anneline her clothes as she passes and finds the sorrowful chick huddled in the armoire. Odette carries it over to the woman. "See? Lethargic."

Immediately the piglet comes to life, wriggling and kicking to get free of the woman's grip.

"Is this what you're missing, little pig?" Odette asks.

She places the chick on the floor. The piglet leaps out of its owner's arms and presses its damp snout to the chick's beak. The chick's feathers fluff. Light returns to the little bird's eyes. The two, piglet and chick, dance around each other, squealing and squeaking.

"Looks like we have found the cause of their sickness," Odette says.

"Like Aline and Valcour when they are reunited," Anneline sighs.

The skinny woman can't speak. She sinks onto the mattress and stretches out her bruised legs. Anneline clears her throat to get Odette's attention and points. A tear tracks down the woman's dirty cheek.

"I can't give you my piglet," she says. "I've lost so much."

"We don't want your piglet," Odette says. "But these two clearly need to be together."

Anneline has dressed quickly and is edging toward the door. *I have to go*, she mouths to Odette. *Renard awaits.*

"I'll take the chick," the skinny woman says.

Odette's heart lurches. She is fond of the chick. And needs it—the chick will one day lay eggs for them. "No."

"Oh, let her take it, Odette," encourages Anneline, eager to get on with her day.

"No," Odette repeats.

"It's just a chick," Anneline says.

Odette thinks fast. "How about we share them?" she suggests. "You have the chick and piglet for one moon. We have them for the next."

"But what about—" the woman says.

"You get most of the coins when the pig goes to market."

The woman mulls this over. "And the—"

"After the pig goes to market, the hen is ours. Its eggs too."

The woman sighs. "Fine."

"And," Odette continues, "you must feed them on time, and talk to them kindly and calmly."

The woman scowls.

"Or no agreement."

The woman's shoulders soften. For a moment she even looks plump. "I'll try."

"Then we have an accord," Anneline proclaims and darts out the door.

Odette glances out the window and down the street to where Renard sits on a low wall, banging his heels against the stones. His hair has been greased, and he wears a dark, moth-eaten cape. When Anneline throws her arms around him, he nearly tumbles backward.

"You take them for the first moon," the tall woman says to Odette, then rushes out the door, clutching a *sou* Odette watched her filch from the mantel. Odette watches out the window as the woman hurries up the street, calling after a fishmonger.

Odette gets to work on her garden bed, clearing weeds and breaking up the soil. The piglet and chick scamper nearby, and Lisane pulls up worms to feed to her new chicks who dawdle after her.

Niçois calls down from the top of the wall. "Your first birth went well, Mother says."

"They have a big family now," Odette answers. "Eight brothers and sisters."

"I wonder what that's like."

Odette has often wished for a sibling or two. Friends whose visits never end.

"Catch!" Niçois drops a small bag from the top of the wall. "We'll eat tomatoes, carrots and courgettes from the same seeds."

Odette opens it. Bounty!

Niçois swings his legs over the wall and leaps down. He squats and raises hillocks in the dirt with his hands.

"There," he says after each one.

Odette pushes a seed into the top and says, "Here."

"There."

"Here."

After they've planted the garden, Niçois has errands to run for his mother.

Odette makes porridge and again studies Mme Geneviève's message.

She thinks about the monk with his humble apologies and the blacksmith with his important capital *B*. She remembers Félix teaching her the capital letters. The letter *I* was an ionic column for a Greek temple. *M* was a bed that a magnificently massive man had slept on, breaking it. *U* was for utensil—a ladle. *S* was a serpent, of course. *T* was a table. *I M-U-S-T*. They spelled a word!

Back upstairs Odette puts the rest of the capital letters in Mms Geneviève's message together.

It makes sense now that the old woman wrote *my apologies humble*—it put the *O* in front of the *U* to spell *YOU*.

I MUST SEE YOU NOW LETTERS

LETTERS is the clue, which leaves....

Without a further thought Odette jumps to her feet and runs down the steps of her home, through the streets of Nevers and to the little shack in the woods.

She knows the way perfectly. As if she has lived in Nevers all her life.

Twenty-One

Mme Geneviève is curled up in bed when Odette enters the cabin. "Are you alone?" she asks Odette.

Her breath is ragged. Odette is taken aback by how weak she looks.

"Yes, I came alone. Were you napping?" Odette asks.

A tear slips from Mme Geneviève's eye. "I have so much to do, but I am tired. I gave my life to the rich, and now I have so little for myself."

Odette straightens Mme Geneviève's blankets. She fills a cup with water and brings it to her, then feeds the oxen and starts a fire to make some broth.

"You know how to work," Mme Geneviève says admiringly. "But sit for a moment, *ma fille*."

Odette draws a chair up to the bed.

"I did not tell the truth the other day," Mme Geneviève begins. "There is a…" She closes her eyes. "Book. Just like my cursed nephew said. Bottom of the oxen's feedbox. Under…"

The old woman's voice fails. Odette holds the cup of water to her lips. Mme Geneviève drinks and again tries to speak. "I worked in big houses. In the book is a story I overheard during my last days as a maid. I hid the book long ago—under that bridge—then looked and looked. For you."

"Me?"

Mme Geneviève grows quiet in her bed. She closes her eyes again. Odette dips a cloth in water and presses it to her forehead.

"Do you have family that I can fetch?" Odette asks. With revulsion she thinks of the yellow-haired man. "Renard…?"

"No!" Mme Geneviève says with surprising strength. "He can't be trusted. He's the one who stole the book from under the bridge. Luckily, the fool left it in a tavern—stopped for a drink on his way home. Always put your address in your books, Odette. If I hadn't, I would never have seen my book again. Ever since then Renard has suspected I have it and has tried to get it from me. But it cannot fall into the wrong hands. A man's life is at stake. Your father—"

Odette is shocked. "My father? His life can't be at stake."

Mme Geneviève squeezes Odette's hand. "No. You're right. He is dead."

"Did you know him?" Questions rush Odette like rain in a sudden storm. But which is the most important one? "What was he like?" she asks.

"I did not know him well. We worked for a short while in the same house. He was helping the master organize his library. He was gentle. He cared about his work. I heard later that he had left a child on this earth when he died. Well, a child in the making. And when I discovered that his cousin…Odette, someone needs you. Terribly."

"*Who*?"

"It's in the book," Mme Geneviève says weakly. "In the feed box. My time on this earth is almost over.

But I'm so happy I found you. Read the book with someone else. Two remember better than one."

Mme Geneviève turns her head to look at Odette. Death blazes, cold, white, in her eyes. Odette gazes back with all the strength she can muster.

"Everything is better with a friend by your side. Do you have a friend?"

Odette shakes her head.

"Not one?"

Odette remembers the girl on the plate, but of course she can't count her as a friend. She is only a picture. Then she remembers how Niçois recognized her in that girl. Niçois sees *her*. Odette. He doesn't care about who she isn't or who she should be— he knows who she *is*. "Yes. I have a friend."

"You will need each other. So you can remember the story." The old woman breathes choppily. Her throat rattles. With supreme effort, she rises up on an elbow. "I want nine bells," she tells Odette. "Tell Father Contrefort. Nine bells. I worked as hard as a man my entire life. Harder, in fact."

Mme Geneviève collapses back onto the mattress. Odette reaches for her hand. It's cold.

Odette lifts the edge of the blanket. Mme Geneviève's feet are cold too, and white as tallow. "Death starts kindly, at the tips," Félix had once explained. "The toes, fingers, ears. Then, like a river, a freezing river, its tributaries move toward the sea: the heart."

Odette rubs Geneviève's hands and feet, but they won't warm. Maybe a song would be comforting? Odette sings through to the end of "*À la claire fontaine.*"

> *I would that the rose*
> *Were still on its briar*
> *And my sweet friend*
> *Still there to love me…*
> *Never will I forget her…*

Mme Geneviève falls deeper into sleep. Her eyes sink. It is as though she is evaporating, Odette thinks, withdrawing from her body. "The body is only a vessel," Félix had once said as a blackbird darted through the graveyard. "Life moves through it."

"Mine too?" Odette had asked, studying her hands, her bruised knees.

Félix stopped digging. He leaned on his shovel. A tear beaded at the corner of his eye. "Yes," he said. "It will pass through your body too. But that is years and years and years away." He put down his shovel and picked her up and placed her feet on his dirty boots. "Of all the people I have known, dearest girl, you are the most alive." Then, down in the fresh, damp grave, he danced a quiet jig, her legs moving in perfect time with his.

Odette smiles, remembering how that dance went on and on. Félix never did anything by half. As they danced, the sun burned through the gray sky, and the two of them laughed, wondering if maybe their dancing had called it out.

Then her mother had come into view, walking toward them with a basket filled with lunch—wine, bread, roast chicken.

Mme Geneviève's breathing quickens. It is as though she's winning a foot race, charging ahead of the others toward the finish line. Her hand lightly squeezes Odette's, a pump, and then her breathing stops. Odette knows there is nothing she can do to change things. She has been in the presence of corpses before. Of course she has—Anneline is her mother, after all, and has the singular talent of creating corpses.

As is the custom, Odette stops the hut's one clock. Then, having no coins and not wanting to rummage in the cupboards like a thief, she arranges the bowls of two spoons over Mme Geneviève's eyes. The tasks buoy her against the unfathomable weight that pulls on her like a tide. Why could she not have met Mme Geneviève sooner? A hardworking woman, an inventor, someone who understood what it was to be adrift without a father...

The oxen make mournful sounds low in their throats, like cats purring sadly. Odette strokes their heads. "Yes, she is gone. I will find a home for you. Don't you fret."

Then Odette climbs through the window into their stable to find the feedbox. She lifts the lid and, after giving each ox a large handful of feed, works her hand through the oats. At the very bottom of the box she touches something unusual. A handle. She pulls, and up comes a small, ornately decorated book.

It is bound with red thread. Odette, with some labor, reads the impressive title:

A Tale Told in the Dining Room
of a Burgundian Mansion
by One Duchess to Another
on a Rainy Afternoon over Glasses of Beaujolais
as Overheard by the Author
Maid and Inventor
Geneviève Pitié

Odette climbs back into the main house. A robin sings on the windowsill near the bed. Odette smiles, imagining it is Mme Geneviève's soul saying goodbye.

She sits on the edge of the bed, lifts the book's cover and begins to read, forgetting for the moment Mme Geneviève's instructions about reading it with a friend.

Enjoy this story, for it is mysterious and true,
and then write the last chapter.

In the county of Jura, a duchess ached
to hold a man in her arms, to nibble on his
earlobes and profess love.

Odette is so engrossed in the book that she does not notice the sound of horse hooves approaching the little house. She reads:

So when a Burgundian duke passed through the Jura, he was invited for supper. He was a fabulous conversationalist, extraordinarily handsome. The duchess sized up his earlobes, touched her tongue to her teeth and began to woo.

Soon she visited the duke in Burgundy. It was a dark night, and she pretended she had gotten lost on her way home from Paris. After supper, when the chateau was dark and everyone slept, the duchess from the Jura crept along the hallways and knocked at his bedroom

"*That* is mine!"

Renard grabs the little book from Odette's hands.

"No!" Odette cries. She tries to tear the book back, but Renard clings to it. His untrimmed fingernails sink into the cover like claws.

Odette is enraged. This book is meant for her! She thinks quickly. Perhaps Renard will weaken when he hears about his aunt. She nods toward Mme Geneviève's body. "Your aunt has…"

Renard barely glances. "Finally. The old ewe is gone."

Odette dives for the book, but Renard turns quickly. His back to her, he leafs through the book's pages frantically. "What? No pictures!"

"She wanted me to have it. It's mine!"

"Well, in her state she won't know if you have it or not, will she?"

"Re-na-ard! Darling!" Anneline is outside the hut, warbling his name. "Did you find the wine?"

Renard shoves the book under his stylish but dirty blouse and hurries to the door to meet Anneline just as she crosses the threshold.

"Renard, my love." Anneline looks into the room. "Daughter! What are you doing here?"

"I was visiting Mme Geneviève. But she has died. Just now."

Anneline crosses herself cursorily. "Poor woman."

Renard dabs at his dry eyes with a fancy, threadbare handkerchief and crumples into Anneline's arms. "My aunt has passed to the other side!" he sobs. Anneline strokes his hair.

Odette watches the two, disgusted. Her eyes move to the bulge where the book is tucked under Renard's shirt. "I will alert the priest and the carpenter," she tells the pair.

Renard raises his head from Anneline's shoulder and, while pretending to blow his nose, gives Odette a cold smile. "Thank you, dear. That would be so nice of you."

Odette walks past the couple, out of the little house and into the spring day. But instead of going to the cathedral to tell Father Contrefort the news, so that the bell ringer can pull the bell ropes and the monks can recite funerary prayers, she sneaks to the back of the little house and finds the door into the oxen's stall. Once inside, she squeezes between the warm beasts and presses up to the window to spy on her mother and Mme Geneviève's dreadful nephew.

Anneline is still comforting Renard. "Shhh. It will be all right," she says, stroking his yellow hair. "Death takes us all." A curate had spoken these exact words when comforting Anneline after her fifth husband, the bank manager, succumbed.

Renard looks up at Anneline. "You are so beautiful," he says.

Anneline giggles. "And you are so handsome!"

"Your eyes."

"Your lips."

"Your shapely calves."

"Your yellow hair."

Odette fights repulsion as the two run their hands over each other. And then—*THUNK*.

"What was that?" Anneline asks.

"Nothing," Renard says. He kicks *A Tale Told in the Dining Room of a Burgundian Mansion* under the bed in which Geneviève still lies. "Only my heart, beating for you."

"Oh, Valcour!"

"Valcour?"

"I mean, Renard!"

As the two fall to the floor, kissing passionately, Odette clambers quietly through the oxen's window back into the house, sinks to her knees and creeps toward them. But just as her fingers touch the book, Renard and Anneline turn and bump into her. Odette freezes. Too late.

"Daughter! I didn't see you there."

"I thought you'd left," Renard says angrily. "Why you—" He swipes at the book in Odette's hands.

"Why are you attacking her?" Anneline asks.

"I'm just teasing her. Poor girl has had a shock today, what with my boring—I mean, dear aunt dying. She needs some cheering up."

"You have a kind heart," Anneline says, kissing the end of Renard's pointy nose and taking his hands firmly in hers.

"Yes. So kind," Odette says. And, gripping the book tightly, she runs out of the little house and into the woods.

"Hey!" Renard calls after. "Hey!"

Odette looks back to see Renard leaping up onto his horse. "Just going to get us some wine," he calls to Anneline. He clicks his tongue and snaps the reins. "*Hue!*"

Odette removes her *sabots* and knots them in her apron along with the book and then tears along the path. As the horse pounds closer and closer, she searches for a tree to climb. Finally the perfect one presents itself. She throws her bundle under a fern and clambers up, branch to branch, as quickly as she can.

She is breathless at the top of a cottonwood tree, hidden by fresh spring leaves, when Renard's horse canters past below.

Twenty-Two

When Odette finds the carpenter, a sinewy man her mother's age, and tells him that Mme Geneviève has died, he grows quiet. "She had many talents," he says. "She was going to invent a tool that let me sharpen all of a saw's teeth at once. That would have saved me so much time."

"She had a long list of things she still wanted to invent."

"I worked alongside her in several large houses. She was a dedicated maid who worked harder than most. But she never boasted. Pine could do for her burial—a modest wood for a modest woman. But I also have this oak coffin here, for sale at a good price. I built it for a man who in fact turned out not to be dead. He had merely fallen into a deep sleep. There is a tiny bit of damage to the inside of the lid, but otherwise it's a lovely coffin, and it has, you could say, the selling point of having been tested."

"Tested?"

"Well, the man was buried for a little while. As the mourners left the gravesite, one heard rapping. Thinking it might be a badger, and thus supper, he investigated and discovered it was something a bit more than a badger. If you look at the lid here, you can see the marks from the man's knuckles, so desperate was his knocking. And there are scratch marks too. See here? I thought they trim the nails of the dead. Clearly, not always."

"Good thing someone heard him," Odette says nervously.

"Yes. The sad thing, though, is he hasn't been quite the same man since he was buried. He is afraid of wood of every kind, which makes life difficult, as you can imagine. Tree or cart wheel, even a twig in a bird's mouth, sends him into a raving panic. He lives in a little stone hut on a rocky hilltop. His wife and children deliver his meals."

"But you are selling it for a low price?"

"Yes. Because of the damage—minor though it is."

At the cathedral, Father Contrefort is again staring sadly at the saints with their missing fingers and noses. He reaches up and strokes the stump of a toe, as if he could make it grow back, then takes out his handkerchief and wipes his eyes. "And they say you can't get water from stone," he jokes.

"Father, I bear sad news. Mme Geneviève the maid has died."

"I am very sorry to hear that. We will ring the bells."

"Her last request was for them to be"—Odette takes a deep breath—"rung nine times."

"*Nine times*? Impossible. It's seven for women. Nine for men. Who, after all, was made of whose rib?"

"Those were her last words. *Nine bells.*"

"Her last words." Father Contrefort strokes his chin.

"Mme Geneviève worked all her life in the houses of the rich. As hard as any man. She was an inventor too. She invented marvelous things."

"Pride is a deadly sin."

"She wasn't proud."

"Invention may be a sin as well. We trust in God to make all things."

"She was creating a liquid that would hold the sun's heat, to release at night and keep people warm."

"That would be against God's wishes."

Odette thought of the nights she and Anneline had shivered in the dark. She thought of various neighbors coughing from the smoke from their fires, and the hours spent getting firewood.

"God wants birds to have their trees, doesn't he?" she asked the priest.

"Yes, indeed."

"But we cut them down for firewood."

"Sunlight is meant for the daytime. If you take some of it away, there won't be enough."

"We sit in shade at the height of day, so there is sunlight to spare."

Father Contrefort looks at Odette with new interest. "You are clever," he says.

"The revolutionaries said men and women were equal—"

The priest's smile fades. He looks at his broken statues. "Don't talk to me about revolutionaries."

A small stone lands at Odette's feet, as if fallen from the sky. She looks up and sees a man's face in a window of the bell tower. He puts a hand out the window and waves, then puts a finger to his lips. His cheeks are wet with tears. He clearly knew, maybe even loved, Mme Geneviève.

Odette, as she runs home, counts as the bells ring. *One, two, three, four, five, six, seven, eight.* Odette waits. *Nine.*

She finds Niçois lying in his yard, drenched with spring sunshine, his dark hair tangled up in the long grass. A ladybug ambles across his chest. Odette positions herself in the sun's path, blocking the light. Niçois, surprised by the sudden shade, opens his eyes.

"I need you," Odette says.

Niçois jumps to his feet. "I am at your service," he says.

Odette indicates the book she has bundled into her apron.

"We need somewhere private to read this," she tells Niçois in a low voice.

"I know the place. My grandparents' old hut!"

Niçois leads Odette down the banks to the rough riverside hut where his father was raised. The hut is nearly lost in overgrown reeds and bushes, and it's filled with rabbits that have made it their home.

They sit on the damp dirt floor, and Odette opens the little book. To her dismay, the first few pages, which she read at Mme Geneviève's house before Renard surprised her, have gone blank. "I see," she says. "This is why we must read the book together. So we can help each other remember it."

For the rest of the afternoon, with wild rabbits sleeping on their laps, amid columns of sunlight that pierce the rotting thatch roof, Odette and Niçois—whose mother taught him to read using midwifery texts—read the book straight through to the end, stopping before turning each page to test each other's memory of it, fixing each word in their minds before it vanishes.

Twenty-Three

—door. The duke answered. He wore pajamas of Lyon silk. The duchess threw her arms around him. "Goodnight to you as well," the duke said, and, before the duchess knew what had happened, he had closed the door. The duchess was back in the hallway, alone. Well, she thought, I guess he is a modest man. Tomorrow I will try again.

She did. After a day of batting her eyes and twirling her umbrella coquettishly as they strolled through the garden, and making deliberate kissing noises as she ate her oysters at supper, she again walked the moonlit *halls of the chateau and knocked at his bedroom door.*

This time he didn't even open the door. "Good night, Duchess!" he called from the other side. "Sleep tight. Don't let the bed lice bite." That, of course, was a joke. There are no lice in a chateau.

The duchess took the joke as an encouraging sign. The duke was simply shy and clearly wanted to have fun with her.

She left the next day feeling hopeful. From her home in the Jura, she sent the duke special cheeses from as far away as Normandy and England, and long letters about nature and the softness of her hair.

She was sure that, with all her beauty and wealth, she could win him. She sent him a bottle of brandy with a pear that had grown inside the bottle. Finally she sent him a painting of herself.

The duke returned the painting, with a note tucked into the frame: I am sorry. I am simply not interested. You seem like a lovely, persistent person. The truth is, I love dukes, not duchesses.

The duchess did not understand the note at all. She flew into a great rage. She tore up her bedsheets and yanked the curtains from their hooks. The next day she consulted a wizard. She wanted revenge.

The wizard gave the duchess a vial of powdered turtle shell and told her to stir the powder into the duke's tea while intoning three times the name of an animal. A few hours after drinking the tea, the duke would turn into the animal she had named.

The duchess visited the duke once again, pretending she was there to make amends. She asked the duke's maids to make tea and set up a table for them on the terrace. "I will pour his tea for him. It is how we apologize in the Jura," she lied.

The duke was nervous. He had heard from a traveling silhouette artist that the duchess had not reacted well to his refusal of her. But he was a dignified man, a true gentleman, too gracious to refuse a cup of tea with anyone. So the two sat together on the terrace, which overlooked a valley, and exchanged pleasantries as the duchess poured the tea.

"And who owns those lands?" the duchess asked, pointing into the distance.

As the duke went to the railing to see which lands she had indicated, the duchess quickly opened the silver vial that hung from her necklace. She emptied the turtle-shell dust into the duke's tea and stirred, whispering, "Donkey, donkey, donkey," inspired by the duke's lovely ears and striking front teeth.

The duchess knocked on the duke's bedroom door late that evening to see if the spell had worked. She heard clomping on the other side of the door, and then a donkey brayed.

Under the spell, the wizard had explained, the duke, now a donkey, would be able to bray only after the sun went down. During the day he would be mute.

To be on the safe side, the wizard had also told the duchess how the spell could be undone.

To be freed from the spell, the new animal would have to be bathed in the water of the oldest well nearby, on the night of a new moon, by someone related to him. The catch was that the spell had to be transferred to someone else before the moon completed its cycle. Some part of the existing animal would have to be ground and stirred into tea, and another animal—any animal—named while it was stirred.

By now, dear Reader, you will have noticed that the words on these pages disappear soon after you have read them. It seems magical, but it is actually not magic. It is science. Chemistry. The ink, which your dear Author created, is a concoction of lemon juice, seawater, aluminium salts and North Sea seal's blood. Once dry, it vanishes if exposed to the air for longer than a minute—giving you just enough time to read a page.

The disappearing ink has been used for obvious reasons: this book must be read only by the reader I choose. If a bad person or a greedy person were to turn the donkey back into a duke, looking for a personal reward, that would put the duke in danger. And the duke, I'm sure we can all agree, has been through enough already.

A final note for you, dear Reader: Someone else has suffered terribly from the duke's disappearance, and that is the tavern owner named Miguel. He and the duke were in love, and Miguel searched for the duke for years. The patrons at his tavern frequently noted how tired he looked in the mornings, for Miguel often searched through the night. Eventually, in sorrow, he closed up the tavern, and at the writing of this, it is not known where he is.

The End

Odette leaves the book open at the last page, and she and Niçois watch as the words *The End* retreat.

Niçois lies back on the grass. "Interesting story," he says.

"It's not just a story," Odette reprimands.

"A man can't be turned into a donkey."

"Is that any stranger than a donkey that only brays after the sun goes down?"

Niçois sits up quickly. "Anne!"

"Yes. And..." Odette takes a deep breath. "There's something I need to tell you. At night Anne cries out that he does not want to be a donkey. That being a donkey is a terrible life."

"You speak *donkey*?"

"No. The donkey speaks Latin. That isn't mentioned in Mme Geneviève's book—so the spell must have gone wrong somehow."

"Why didn't you tell me?"

"It seemed impossible. Imagine what you would have thought! A girl saying she can understand a donkey's brays."

"I would have believed you," Niçois says. And Odette believes him in turn.

"Mme Geneviève mentioned a cousin of my father's, and my mother has always said my father had a drop of royal blood in his veins. The duke and my father were cousins, I think, which means I'm related to him too! From what the book says, I'm the only one who can rescue the duke."

"So your father isn't still alive?"

Odette shakes her head. "My mother—" No. She did not have to tell Niçois, not yet, at least, that her mother was an accidental serial murderer. "He died."

"I'm sorry."

"I never met him. So it doesn't really matter, does it?"

"That makes two of us without a father."

"Half orphans," Odette says. "It's funny. Even though I never met my father, I feel as though I knew him. I remember once running a fingernail under his thumbnail as he told me a story and digging out a spiral of dirt." It is the first time she has told anyone this memory, and soon as the words are in the air she realizes with a start that she isn't remembering her father. She's remembering Félix. Her heart swells with thudding grief.

SNAP.

Something cracks outside the hut, as if someone has stepped on a stick. Odette and Niçois freeze. The rabbits go on alert, ears high.

When a magpie hops in through the hut's small door, mayhem erupts—rabbits leaping, the magpie flapping wildly, cawing and crashing into walls before darting up the chimney hole into the sky.

Niçois smiles, relieved. "Well? Let's go break a spell! Let's meet your royal relative!"

The two tear through town, arriving out of breath to find Anne standing sleepily under his tree.

Odette tries to explain in Latin about the spell. *Vos adjuvare possumus.* "We can help you," she pants. "Tonight, in the darkness of the new moon, we'll lead you to a well and bathe you. We'll take hair from your tail to grind for tea so someone else can become an animal." *Vos cognoscimus.* "We know who you are! You'll be freed from being a donkey at last."

Anne raises his head and looks at her. His eyes busily study her lips. He seems to understand, at least, that something exciting is happening. He takes several steps forward and then elegantly bends a leg and dips. He trots right, then right again.

"The *sarabande!*" Odette laughs.

Niçois throws his arms around the animal's neck. "I knew you were special," he cries.

But as quickly as the donkey's spirits buoyed, menace seems to take hold. His ears press low to his head, and he growls deep in his throat.

Twenty-Four

As Odette climbs the stairs to her small house to make her mother's supper and prepare for the night's exciting chore, she hears familiar screeching. "He is *my husband*. And you. You, with your cloak—"

"It's all I have, " Anneline says meekly. "And it is full of holes."

"Your airs then. You have lots of those."

"I did not know. I never would have—"

Odette darts up the stairs and finds her mother pressed against the wall, a skinny woman thrusting a necklace in her face. "He gave me this gift," the woman says. "Ivory and silver. Is this not a sign of true love?"

"It's lovely. An object of beauty," Anneline says as she surreptitiously works a bracelet of fake silver over her hand and drops it to the floor.

"I could strangle you with it."

"*Madame!*" Odette shouts.

The woman turns and gawps.

"My mother didn't steal your pig, and she didn't steal your husband."

"She and Renard don't even live together," Anneline appeals to Odette. "He's been away from Nevers for years, living on the edge of Paris."

The skinny woman shrugs. "Marriages go through difficult patches."

"Ten years is a long 'patch,'" Anneline says.

Odette turns to the skinny woman. "Leave."

"Your mother is a witch. You know that, don't you? A jezebel."

"She is my mother. That is what I know."

The woman backs down the stairs. "I'll be back for the chick and piglet. It is my turn to keep them."

Anneline falls onto the bed. Tears trickle from her eyes and pool in her ears. Odette sits down beside her.

Then something strange happens.

Anneline reaches for Odette's hand and squeezes. "I'll try to be better," she says.

Odette would like to believe her mother, but Anneline has caused her so much woe. She seemed to be changing, but this terrible Renard. Such an obvious scoundrel. How could her mother have fallen for him?

She can't help remembering, though, Anneline's insistence on posting her notice in every new town. On never forgetting the promise of that empty box under the bridge. If Anneline hadn't persisted...

The old could spring anew, it was true. Félix, studying a grave he had just filled, had once said, "If you didn't know any better, you would think it was a fresh garden bed."

Odette returns her mother's squeeze. She is grateful that Anneline does not squeeze again, does not turn the moment into a silly game.

"Did you count my toes when I was born?" Odette asks.

"Oh yes. And your fingers. You had ten of each."

"I still do."

"That is good to know."

Twenty-Five

I n the early evening, as soon as the sun goes down, Anne brays. This time his brays are unusually loud and boisterous. Odette listens closely. *Non dubitate, fortuna fatum vobis exonerabit.* "Do not doubt that fortune will lighten your fate. Fate is vain, yes, and resolute. But Fortune—Fortune dazzles." *Fortuna cursum temporis mutat.* "Fortune changes the course of time. Fortune is fate's comeuppance."

After serving her mother a supper of oatmeal, with spinach gathered from the overgrown garden outside the riverside hut, Odette tucks her mother into bed under the knitted blanket, along with *Aline et Valcourt.* Odette herself is too nervous to eat. She feeds the chickens and the piglet, does some knitting, then leaves Anneline, saying she is going out to fetch water. She knows that her mother, who does not understand the nature of chores, will never wonder at her fetching water after nightfall.

Odette takes the mended bucket with her.

Once in the street she whistles toward Niçois's open window a tune they devised as a signal. It is a magpie's cry. Low gobbling in the throat and then a high-pitched whistle. Niçois hurries silently out of his house to the road.

"I stuffed my bed," he whispers excitedly. "With my shape."

The night resounds with Anne braying mournfully.

"What is he saying?" Niçois ask.

Odette translates: "I was wrong." *Fortuna caligo est.* "Fortune is mist. It is helpless against the sharp-nosed fox that leads you to your final den. Fate is cruelly sure of its destination. Fortune is lost." Odette is puzzled. "He is back to his glum habits. Earlier he was quite excited."

The two are soon in sight of the chestnut tree, but there's no sign of the donkey.

"He's gone!" Niçois gasps. It's true. Anne's triangle of grass is empty. "All my life, Anne has stood here," Niçois cries.

Odette and Niçois run through the streets, asking the few people up at that hour—the lamp extinguisher, the flag mender—if they have seen Anne. They haven't. Odette and Niçois follow a light in the distance. The blacksmith is still awake, banking his coals for the night.

"Did you see Anne, the donkey?" they pant. "He is not in his place!"

"I saw only a man with a pointed nose. He begged me to make him the sharpest pin in the world. That's what he said. *The sharpest pin in the world.* He muttered that a halter would not do the trick, that he was dealing with a very stubborn animal. Perhaps he meant Anne. He showed me three silver coins in the palm of his hand. But when it came time to pay, he only gave me one. Still, I made a *sou.* I did a very good job, of course. My brother always said that any job worth doing should be done well."

"Did he have a beard?" Odette asked.

"My brother?"

"No. The man who wanted the sharp pin."

"Yes. A silly Paris beard."

"And buckles on his shoes?"

"Silly buckles."

"Renard," Odette says. "Bad to the bone. The marrow. He's jabbing Anne along against his will with a pin!" She mouths to Niçois: *He's figured out the spell.*

"*The sharpest pin in the world,*" the blacksmith repeats. "I wouldn't have done it if I had known. Believe me. There is already too much pain in the world. You know these things when you have lost a brother."

Odette feels as though she is going to faint. Her heart throbs like a bruise. She wants to lie down right there and sob in the firelight. She has no idea why. Niçois catches her elbow as her knees weaken. "It must be that I haven't eaten much today," Odette says, trembling.

"This will help," the blacksmith says. He opens a cloth and gives her a lump of cheese, which he cuts with a knife with a wooden handle.

"Olive wood," Odette says, surprised.

"Yes," says the blacksmith. His eyes are dark and knowing and kind. And so familiar. Odette's knees wobble again. Her heart surges. Why?

"Thank you," she whispers. The blacksmith smiles, watching her eat.

Odette's ears perk up. "Listen!"

Anne is braying in the distance. *Dolor acer est!* "Pain is sharp or dull. But it is always a cruel master."

Odette and Niçois run out of the blacksmith's shop and toward the cries. On the crest of a hill outside of town, silhouetted under starlight, they spy Anne, followed by a scrawny man who can only be Renard. He has one hand on a rope around Anne's neck, and in his other hand Odette thinks she sees the glint of his violent weapon.

Odette and Niçois run quickly, Niçois leading the way. Finally they are so close they can hear Renard swearing. He is consumed by fury and does not notice their approach. On the count of three, the two leap on him. Niçois grabs his wrist, and Odette wrests the pin from his hand and throws it into a cornfield.

They knock Renard down onto the road. Odette sits on his chest, and Niçois holds his legs. Renard's yellow hair is askew, and a buckle is now missing from one of his shoes. He begins to sob. "I heard you in the hut by the river, reading the book! I know the story now."

Odette remembers the branch snapping. So that was him, not the magpie.

"But this donkey is nothing but a donkey," Renard whines. "I've bathed him in every old well in this town, and he remains an ass."

Odette strokes Anne's belly. "Don't worry. We'll save you," she says.

Anne presses his head into her chest and huffs. Then he nudges her out of the way and sits squarely on Renard.

"Hold him there!" Niçois yells. He undoes the rope from around Anne's neck, and he and Odette use it to lash the yellow-haired man to a willow tree.

"Why would you hurt an innocent animal?" Niçois demands.

"And take something that isn't yours," Odette adds, tightening the knot. "And be such a neglectful nephew?"

"Well, she was an ugly aunt," Renard says, yawning.

"You have no heart," Odette says.

But Renard has fallen asleep standing, tied in place.

Niçois and Odette study Anne, who is nibbling the grass at his feet. Odette unwinds from her waist a rope she knitted earlier in the evening. "Now," she whispers.

In a flash she and Niçois wrap the rope tightly around Anne's jaw and head, fashioning a halter and reins. The poor animal is terrified and in some pain from the snug bonds, but Odette and Niçois simply can't afford to have him bray as they lead him through town. They can't chance a crowd following them, or another greedy gold seeker interfering. They explain this to Anne, and while he does not understand what they say, the kindness in their voices calms him.

Niçois and Odette lead Anne to four of the oldest wells Niçois can think of and dowse him in water, but he stubbornly remains a donkey. As they pull him through starlit fields and forest, they discuss who, if they are successful in breaking the spell, they will change into an animal in his place.

Niçois argues for Renard. "He's a villain. It is clear as day. Jabbing a donkey all night with a sharp pin!"

"Perhaps." Odette remembers Anneline's distress the night before. "How about the skinny lady with the piglet? We could turn *her* into a piglet." But her heart isn't in it. "It's a terrible thing to do to a person really."

Niçois plunks himself down on a rock. "Perhaps this isn't going to work," he says. He sounds to Odette as if he is on the verge of tears. "Maybe Mme Geneviève was being fanciful or got the spell wrong."

Odette looks at Anne, noticing again his regal, dignified bearing. "We have to keep trying," she says. "We have to look around every corner."

"I suppose there could be surprises," Niçois says slowly. "After all, you and I did not know of each other until last moon. We each had no idea the other existed, and now we are like peas in a pod. Like—"

"Brother and sister."

Niçois smiles. "Yes." He stands. "All right. Let's keep on. Until dawn."

"Hope springs eternal," Odette says. The polyglot had quoted the poem often. Odette recites from it:

Hope springs eternal...
The soul, uneasy, and confined from home
rests and wanders in a life to come...

Anne sighs. Poetry is something he understands. Odette strokes his neck. "*Your* soul certainly knows about being confined."

"My friend!" M. Mains barrels around the corner and throws his arms around Anne's head. He's jolly. "What are you doing, roaming the streets in the dark with these two? And what is this contraption around your head? Never mind. I have just had the luck to smell the young palms of the baker's assistant. Butter and yeast. We rarely remember that our bread is made in the night, while the stars gleam."

M. Mains looks at Odette. "I remember you. The message from the old woman. But you haven't allowed me to smell your hands."

Odette wrings her hands nervously. Niçois steps forward, offering his. "You can smell mine."

M. Mains gives them a sniff. "Donkey, well water. I'm not sure I can make sense of that."

"Maybe you can help us," Odette says. She looks at Niçois, who nods. "But you must keep a secret."

"I love secrets. There are smells on hands that I have never spoken of aloud. Smells that speak of passion and failed alchemy."

As Odette explains their mission, M. Mains grows excited. He pats Anne on the head. "Hello in there, Duke!" he tells him. "I always thought you had a majestic scent. Imagine! One day we will sit together and cross our human legs and share a glass of Saint-Véran Chardonnay with its citrus notes and honeysuckle aroma. We will chat! Man to man."

His face crinkles in thought. It then opens. "Mme Source! She really is a marvel. Her hands smell of this place with a perfection I have known nowhere else."

Odette remembers M. Mains mentioning the woman when they met by the river. "She smells of boeuf bourguignon."

"Yes."

"And she can help us?"

"She is a dowser and the child of a dowser. A diviner."

"I know her," Niçois says. He sounds excited. "People pay her to find water underground, so they know where to dig for a well. She uses the forked branch of a hazelnut tree."

"Yes," M. Mains says. "But she says it's not the hazel wood that helps her so much, though everyone likes to believe that it is. It's science—her understanding of plants and trees. Some grow where water is plentiful, others where it isn't. Dips in the land can indicate water. Mme Source will know all the nearby water channels. And I appreciate any opportunity to visit her. Please, follow me."

As they set off, at a brisk pace, M. Mains tells them more about Mme Source. "She is the oldest woman in Nevers. She is layered like a pearl onion. I am very fond of being in her company."

"Will she mind us waking her?" Odette asks.

"Not for something this important."

Mme Source opens the door of her well-kept cottage, wearing a nightgown and holding a candle.

She doesn't seem surprised by the strange group in front of her. Odette wonders if it's because she's so old and has seen so much.

"Yes?" she says.

M. Mains takes her hands and breathes in excitedly. "Marjoram, rosemary, thyme, sage. And— is that—mint?"

Mme Source laughs. "Yes. I gardened late into the evening."

"Your hands," M. Mains sighs, "are a bouquet. A banquet. A history book."

Mme Source laughs again.

Odette lightly jabs M. Mains with her elbow.

"Right. Where were we?" M. Mains says. "We need your help," he tells Mme Source. "But you must swear yourself to secrecy. At least until the sun rises. Then the secret will be out! This donkey is not as he appears, and these young people are looking for the oldest well in Nevers so that his true self can be revealed."

Odette explains the spell, and Mme Source considers Anne. "This does make sense. All your braying, your refusal to lie down in the muck. Your dance steps. Well, if it means you will stop moaning all night, then I will help."

She thinks for a moment. "I know of two wells you have not yet tried."

"Marvelous." M. Mains swoons. He takes Mme Source's left hand in his and boldly kisses it.

"It will smell of your lips," Mme Source teases.

She excuses herself to get dressed. She then steers the group through a field filled with shadowy, sleeping hogs to a well thick with vines. They draw up the bucket, sprinkle some of the water onto Anne and wait. He remains the same.

"One more," Mme Source says, this time piloting the group into a small copse of elm trees, at the center of which is a little door in the ground. "It is snug," she says, tugging on it, "as though it hasn't been opened in a hundred years. I doubt the yellow-haired man was here earlier." She drops a stone in. A little splash resonates in the deep dark. But after the effort of lowering and raising the bucket, Anne remains a donkey.

Everyone except Anne falls to the ground, exhausted, dispirited. A rooster crows in the distance.

The sky exchanges black for dark blue. Odette, lying on her side, feels as though she might cry. The world is waking up, and they have failed to release the duke from the spell.

Then she hears a stream trickling not far away. She listens closely and imagines the water burbling and bubbling, its currents braiding, the small river constantly transforming. *Eureka!* Her *nous* feels as though it has been doused in freezing water. She leaps up, vivified. "The water that runs under the cathedral!"

Mme Source sits up in a flash and nods her great head of white hair. "Yes! My dear, that is it. Of course!"

Twenty-Six

Halfway to the cathedral Odette stops in her tracks. On the Pont de Tour, just up ahead, Renard and her mother are locked in an argument. Renard has managed to get free of the rope somehow, and he looks pathetic. Beaten. He sits on the bridge wall, banging his heels against its side, hanging his head, his hair greasy and askew.

"You could have told me that you're married!" Anneline is shouting.

"She means nothing to me," Renard insists. "She is never happy. Believe me. You are the only one. Please hold my hand. You're all I have."

But Anneline refuses. She smacks Renard's hand out of the way just as Anne notices the yellow-haired man and charges, braying fiercely.

Renard looks up so suddenly that he loses his balance. He tumbles backward, over the bridge rail and out of sight, shouting as he goes down, "Paris buckles!" Then there is a loud crack, and all is silent.

"No!" Anneline peers over the side of the bridge. "I should have held his hand when he wanted me to!"

A wiry man pushing a cart loaded with jugs appears at her side in the twilight. "Madame, I saw everything." It is Guillaume, the painter, on his way to work. "I know you did not push him. I mean, you had him up against the wall, perhaps, but really, he had himself up against the wall. I mean, you cannot pretend you are not married when you are. Madame, yes, cry into my shoulder. There, there."

Odette runs to Anneline, who gives her a strange look. It is a look Odette has not seen before. Anneline looks sorry. Even ashamed. She wipes her nose on Guillaume's shoulder. "I've done it again, daughter. Dove into a rabbit hole that leads nowhere. The only time I got it right was with Félix." Anneline's eyes water. "I dove in with Félix, but I could see. You'd think it would have been dirt and darkness with him, but it was water and light."

"That sounds like love," Guillaume murmurs.

"Is that what it was?" Anneline asks.

Niçois pulls on Odette's elbow. "We need to hurry," he whispers. "M. Mains and Mme Source have gone ahead with Anne. Your mother will be fine with the painter."

Niçois grabs Odette's hand and starts to run. Odette, hesitant at first, soon runs along with him. He holds her hand so tightly she feels anchored in place, even as they fly through the streets of Nevers. She thinks of the baby delivered the night before, who before long will run through these same streets—as a boy or a girl, whatever she or he chooses. Maybe both at once! She wonders at that. In Nevers, it seems, each child can be who they truly are. "This way," Mme Source whispers once they are gathered outside the cathedral. She convoys the group to a side door that is hidden in the shadow of a flying buttress. "Try not to get noticed."

Odette laughs nervously. "Not get noticed? Walking into a church with a donkey?"

"Act like Anne is supposed to be here. Hold your head high."

Mme Source leads everyone to a plaque on a wall extolling the brilliant career of Antoine-Philippe Sournois, Mayor of Nevers, 1723–1729. "This has been here for seventy years," she explains. "But it is not just a plaque. It is a screen, blocking the entrance to the old baptismal pool. For our interests, it's a portal. The water that runs under the city rises up in this spot, constantly refilling the pool."

"A spring," M. Mains murmurs. "Splendid."

"A flowing artesian well. The cathedral was built around it, and for hundreds and hundreds of years the people of Nevers were baptized in its active waters."

"Why would they stop?" Odette asks. She has never been baptized herself, since Anneline holds the radical notion that no one should be baptized without choosing to be. Odette can decide for herself at any time now that she's old enough.

"The mayor bought into a business that made baptismal fonts—stone bowls on stands.

He convinced the bishop that the water in a standing font would be easier to consecrate. With fresh water constantly bubbling up into the pool, a priest couldn't keep up with blessing it, he argued. The bishop fell for his argument—even though it means a monk must top up the bowl every day with water drawn from a well down the road, and the water gets stagnant and thick. Now get your fingers behind this plaque. And pull."

Odette, Niçois, M. Mains and Mme Source haul on the plaque. But it doesn't budge.

"It's impossible," M. Mains puffs.

A chorus of voices rises up behind them. "We can help."

Odette turns, surprised to see a trio of vagrants rise from a nearby pew, rubbing sleep from their eyes. "We have heard the pool burbling in our dreams. And we crave a good bath."

"Baths are important," M. Mains says. "Just don't wash your hands too well."

"The pool should never have been closed," says one of the trio, a woman with a nest of gray hair. "That mayor was greedy, not religious. He sold dozens of fonts. You will see them at the church in Dijon, and Macon, even in the great abbey of Cluny. He lined his pockets, he did. While shutting off nature." The woman digs her thick fingers behind the plaque. "Heave!"

"Watch your toes!" M. Mains yells.

But even with seven people pulling, using all their strength, the plaque only jiggles on its bolts and then settles right back into its spot.

Anne pushes through the work gang. He shakes his head, which makes the reins on the halter fling left and right.

"Yes!" Odette says.

She loops the reins around the corners of the plaque, and Anne, with Herculean strength, pulls backward, once and for all loosening the great brass plate from the wall.

It clangs to the floor.

The group peers at a small pool of clear water, bordered on all sides by rock. Plants grow where sunlight has reached through chinks in the walls. The water moves and swirls. The sound is like music.

"Beautiful," murmurs the woman with the nest of gray hair.

"*Hé, là!*" A priest charges toward the crew. "What are you doing?"

Odette pushes Anne toward the water. "Get in!"

Anne leaps into the pool with astonishing grace.

As soon as his front hooves touch the water, he starts to change. His hooves stretch and separate —into fingers and toes. His belly recedes into a man's firm chest. His ears shrink.

"Ooh!" The small crowd swoons.

"The hair!" Odette yelps. Just as Anne dips the top of his head into the water, Odette tears out a handful of the donkey's tail.

A moment later an extraordinarily handsome man rises from the water. In place of a mane, he has long, flowing hair.

Mme Source falls to her knees. "The lost duke!"

M. Mains throws his hat to the man so he can cover his family jewels.

"Yes. It is me," I say.

Epilogue

Yes, dear Reader, I, the duke, now freed from the shape of a donkey, have been your narrator.

Those first moments in the cathedral were truly extraordinary. It felt as though the universe had shuddered and filled me anew. And although my body felt bruised all over, it was pure joy to be embraced by my courageous second cousin, Odette, and her loving friend Niçois. The priest fainted at the sight of my transformation. The pew sleepers, after getting over their shock, bathed in the waters, wondering if they might be changed as well. M. Mains smelled my hands, pronouncing the scent "unclassifiable, indefinable, shorn of the past, dukish."

A moon has waxed and nearly fully waned again since that momentous dawn. I have not only returned to my house but have also found, in a nearby town, my love Miguel, who had never given up hoping I would return. An astounding gardener and cook, he has filled our pantry and larder with dry sausages, cured ham, jams, cheeses, and vegetables preserved in vinegar. We have been feasting.

Yes. *We.*

Odette and Anneline have moved in with us. Lisane and her brood of chicks too, along with the piglet. And Mme Geneviève's oxen. I do not mind animals in my house. Before I was a donkey, I would have. But during all those years in my mucky field, how I wished someone would invite me into their home.

Renard didn't survive his fall off the bridge. He cracked his head open and drowned. As soon as he was dead, his wife, the skinny woman in the pinafore, grew light on her feet and a calm spread over her face. She has moved into the little stone house over the road, and the piglet and chick—now pig and hen—visit her often, walking between our houses, the hen sometimes riding on the pig's back.

Now, you may have wondered at Odette's wobbly knees when the blacksmith looked into her eyes. And at her reaction to the olive-wood handle of his knife. Maybe you noticed that the blacksmith mentioned a brother.

Well, while Odette was at the blacksmith's buying a candlestick seven days ago, he again mentioned his brother, only this time by name: Félix. Yes. The Félix Odette knew and loved as a girl, the Félix who loved Anneline and whom Anneline loved back. The blacksmith, Clément, has since been to tea several times. When she is with him, Anneline's voice deepens. It seems to take root.

The marvelous thing is, Clément has cheated death impossibly often. Once, as he rode in a carriage, the horses drawing it were spooked by a wolf, and the carriage tumbled down a hill. Everyone—horses, driver—died, except for Clément. Another time, Clément found himself in a duel, but his opponent sneezed just as they were about to shoot and fell into a ditch, shooting himself instead. As Clément was fighting some Austrians one winter, a musket ball meant for him was intercepted by a robin that flew into its path. There is no doubt he will be safe with Anneline.

It is a good thing that Odette has a good ear for language and so learned Latin. She tells me that my speaking Latin wasn't mentioned in Mme Geneviève's book. We believe there was a mistake made when the duchess cast the spell. Perhaps she sneezed or coughed. Who knows? But it was a lucky mistake for me.

It is wonderful to be a man again, to be able to scratch and reach upward and to talk and talk and talk. Despair still assails me some nights, but I do not shout out in Latin, at least, and there is Miguel to curl up to. I have faith the unfathomable loneliness will pass in time.

Finally, when the sun gives way today to a moonless night, M. Gustave will get his greatest wish.

Tonight, in the early summer of 1799, while the people of Nevers sleep in their beds, Odette will pour M. Gustave a cup of tea, and the largest chicken that ever lived will leap into the air and flap its great wings. It will fly over the marketplace, over the cathedral, over the garden beside a little house where M. Mains and Mme Source hold hands in the starlight, over the little house on the bridge and over this great home in the forest.

Up, up, up, the great chicken will fly, receding into the sky over the town that has become Odette's and Anneline's home. They have no plans to leave Nevers. They will stay. *Always.*

· THE END ·

Author's Note

In the late 1700s in France, the divide between rich and poor was extreme. Though they made up only 2 percent of the population, the nobility and the Catholic Church held all the power. The church ran the hospitals and schools, while the nobility controlled the government, the army and the court of the extravagant and ineffectual King Louis XVI. The remaining 98 percent was made up of the bourgeoisie, some of whom owned land and businesses; artisans and farmers, who scraped by day to day; and the very poor, who scrounged to survive. All were judged by the priests and bishops and heavily taxed by the nobles, who paid no taxes themselves.

Inspired by modern ideas about liberty and equality, people rose up in the early summer of 1789. On July 14 they stormed the Bastille, the fortress-like armory and prison in Paris, freeing prisoners and taking weapons and gunpowder. While they made their demands peacefully at first, violence became necessary.

Things became very violent from 1793 to 1794, a time now called the Reign of Terror, during which over 16,500 of the wealthy and resistant were sentenced to death, often by guillotine, a blade that swiftly sliced off their heads. Many argued that the guillotine was humane compared to the torture and poverty that prisoners and commoners suffered under the monarchy. The Revolution occurred mostly in the big cities of France, such as Paris and Lyon.

The Revolution went on for about a decade. It was a period of exhilarating freedom, horrendous violence and great instability. Although Napoleon Bonaparte took power in 1799, calling himself Emperor, the egalitarian ideals of the French Revolution endured and spread throughout Europe and around the world, leading to many freedoms we enjoy today. Bastille Day, celebrated every July 14, is France's biggest holiday.

Nevers is a real city in Burgundy, on the Loire River, with a cathedral with fabulous flying buttresses and a sixth-century baptistery that, after having been shut up for centuries, was exposed to the light by World War II bombing.

Pierre Gaspard Chaumette was born in Nevers in 1763, into a family of shoemakers, and rose to become a surgeon. His anti-religious ideals—he once referred to Christians as "enemies of reason"—set him at odds with the God-fearing revolutionary leader Maximilien Robespierre. He was accused, most likely falsely, of being part of a plot to overthrow Robespierre and was beheaded in 1794.

While many facts in the novel are true—for example, the Loire Bridge was half stone and half wood for the better part of a decade, and Nevers is famous for its *faïence* dishes—I have taken many liberties. I do not know whether Robespierre ever visited Nevers, for example. Some cultural lore, such as spankings with nettles and three washdays named Purgatory, Hell and Heaven, is borrowed from *The Horse of Pride*, Pierre-Jakez Hélias's 1975 memoir of growing up in Brittany, a region very far from Burgundy.

As for the name of the city, it has nothing to do with the English meaning. It evolved from the town's early Celtic-Latin name, Noviodunum, meaning "hill fort," which over time became Nevirnum and, finally, Nevers.

I started to write the novel after a visit to Nevers. At the time, I was reading *The Discovery of France*, by Graham Robb, about how truly quirky and diverse France remained despite the unifying force of the Revolution. Robb writes of a "vast encyclopedia of micro-civilizations...a land in which mule trains coincided with railway trains, and where witches and explorers were still gainfully employed when Gustave Eiffel was changing the skyline of Paris."

Finally, this novel was inspired by a donkey that spent its days under a tree in the small town of La Roche Vineuse, Burgundy, where my family and I spent several months when my children were young. The donkey often brayed at night persistently. One night, woken again, I groggily asked my partner, "What does he want?"

His response was immediate: "To not be a donkey."

Halfway through writing the novel, while researching *faïence*, I came upon the plate below for sale on eBay. It was made in Nevers around the time Odette would have run through its streets. I promptly bought it, grateful for the crack that made it affordable.